HUNT
THE HUNTER

HUNT
THE HUNTER

•

Jeff R. Spalsbury

AVALON BOOKS
NEW YORK

Published by Avalon Books,
an imprint of Thomas Bouregy & Co., Inc.
160 Madison Avenue, New York, NY 10016

Library of Congress Cataloging-in-Publication Data

Spalsbury, Jeff R.
   Hunt the hunter / Jeff R. Spalsbury.
      p.   cm.
   ISBN 978-0-8034-7710-0
   1. Guerrillas—Fiction.   2. United States—History—Civil War,
1861–1865—Veterans—Fiction.   I. Title.
   PS3619.P335H86 2010
   813'.6—dc22

                                                      2010022407

PRINTED IN THE UNITED STATES OF AMERICA
ON ACID-FREE PAPER
BY HADDON CRAFTSMEN, BLOOMSBURG, PENNSYLVANIA

To Lisa and Sara,
daughters extraordinary and treasured

Acknowledgments

I would like to give special thanks to Joy Ann Fischer, editor and friend, who made sure all my horses were taken care of properly and that I was always pointed in the right direction, on or off the horse; Tommy Vegas and Stan Leach, gone too soon; Ralph and Ruben de la Rosa, Americans who bring honor to their Mexican heritage, and to all the other de la Rosas and Morales who shared with me their love, food, laughter, and how to party; Jerry Bailey, whose stories of his youth made their way in; Charles H. McMakin III (Mac) and Donna McMakin, Mac is a real sheriff (now retired) and Donna is a real sheriff's wife, and they are real friends; Vince McGuire, who wouldn't mind getting the salary of a bank vice president; Barry A. Metzler, who is a bank vice president and has taken me on some wild rides; and to Larry A. Swartz, friend, confidant, co-conspirator at the 3020 Club, and a dear and special buddy who has been there for me since the third grade.

Chapter One

As he came closer to the town of Quiet Valley, Dave Kramer felt the bone-aching weariness of his long journey fade as he neared home. His horse, sensing the anticipation of her rider, picked up her pace. Still, Dave rode with the wariness of a man who hadn't quite accepted that his years of fighting a war were over.

Sweat trickled down his face, cleared off a narrow groove of dust, and then dropped silently away as more trail dust coated the moist channel. He paid little attention to the sweat or the dust but let his dark brown eyes absorb landscape he'd thought he would never see again. Stretching before him was a calico patchwork of pines and aspen, framed by lofty Colorado mountains laced with white fingers of snow.

He was more than six feet tall, wiry, with strong, agile muscles, broad shoulders, and a face women observed with a nod of pleasure. His eyes could be gentle or hard, but it had been a long time since he'd allowed them to look gently out onto the world.

The horse waded across a stream and headed down a seldom-used mountain pass toward the small town waiting among the aspen that grew abundantly in the middle of the long valley. Twice Dave almost left the trail to visit old friends whose homes he saw in the distant foothills, but he wanted to see Betty and his father first—plenty of time to visit others later.

Once out of the pass, he veered over to the main road leading into town. Soon he approached a small grove of cottonwood trees behind the combination bank and hotel. The bank-hotel was a huge two-story structure built right in the center of the road—so much so that the road split around it on both sides and then resumed as one again in the front of the building.

He wondered at the empty corral behind the hotel but shrugged it from his mind and rode quickly around the building.

Dave pulled his horse to a sudden halt and gaped at Main Street. He squeezed his eyes shut and shook his head, trying to erase what he couldn't believe. He stared again with intensifying bewilderment. There didn't seem to be a single person in the town. The streets were barren, no horses tied to the rails, no one walking, no children playing, no dogs sleeping in the sun. "Where is everyone?" he mumbled to himself and his horse. A single tumbleweed bounced erratically before him, kicking up small dust puffs.

He rode a little farther and stopped again. He could see into some of the dusty store windows, and nothing moved. He looked up at the rooftops, between the buildings—nothing. Just silence. He saw no wagon tracks, no hoof tracks, no boot tracks. The dusty street was as smooth as a still pond in the late afternoon. The silence was unsettling. No murmur of voices, no sounds of horses, no dogs barking, no children crying.

"My God, Chocolate," he muttered, more to himself than to the horse. "It's a ghost town."

The town did indeed have a weary, graveyard look.

Dave urged Chocolate down the street. The Queen Bee was motionless—no rattle of whiskey bottles, no click of poker chips, no quick purr of cards being shuffled in the hands of a gambler. Dust darkened every window. He fought his fear, hoping what he saw was just his imagination, a crazy, hideous nightmare.

Ahead, the door of the pharmacy banged softly in the wind but didn't latch. Except for the gentle banging sound and the low murmur of an irregular breeze, the town made no noise.

Dave stared at the sign outside a building at the end of the street. THE QUIET VALLEY WEEKLY. He dismounted stiffly from his long ride and tied Chocolate to the hitching post. The front door was unlocked. Dave walked in, tempted to pull his Adams from its holster but somehow knowing it would be unnecessary. Dust covered the two desks, which otherwise looked just as they had when he left so long ago. He walked back to the handpress and gazed at it lovingly. His fingers moved gently over the black metal frame, a hint of printer's ink still in the air. For a moment, he forgot the emptiness of the town. His memory soared back to his youth and the good times he'd had with his father, running the press.

He looked back at the larger desk and wondered where his father was and what had happened to him. He opened the door that led to their living quarters, but it was as empty as the front.

He stalked out of the newspaper office and stared up and down the street in stunned silence. Finally, he crossed the street into the Queen Bee. A long, low building, it was the only saloon in town.

It, too, was empty and dusty. He walked across musty sawdust to the bar and found a bottle of whiskey hidden underneath it. His father had pointed it out to him with a chuckle because all the townspeople knew where Andy kept the good stuff, and they also knew that the strangers who traveled through got the cheap swill. He deftly popped the cork and found a clean but dusty glass. He poured the liquor into it, swished it around, threw the liquid to the floor, and filled it again. He drank it in two quick swallows and savored the burning sensation it gave him. The empty tables with their covering of dust seemed to mock him. This was wrong, all wrong.

Dave was nineteen when he'd left for the war. Except for a few trips throughout the Colorado Territory, he had not traveled much before then. Now he felt he had traveled too much and seen too much. He had turned twenty-three three days after the war ended, yet he felt much older. He carried his Adams a trifle low and had used it often, too often. He had fought for the North as a guerrilla, a spy. He was supposedly on the winning side, but war always hurt both sides, no matter the victor.

Before the war, all he'd thought about was working at his father's newspaper, content that he would take his father's place as publisher when he got older. That had changed in 1861 when the Southern states declared themselves independent by secession and formed the Confederate States of America. On April 12, the

day he turned nineteen, the bombardment of Fort Sumter occurred, although it would be a week before Quiet Valley heard
about it.

In late July, after the battle at Bull Run in Virginia, the soldiers
from the small fort outside Livermore rode into town and asked
for volunteers. He signed up, returned to the office, and told his
father. Robert Kramer wasn't angry, only sad at the chance of losing his son. Dave remembered how his father had placed his hands
on his shoulders and said that a man must always do what he
thought was right.

Dave shook his head, poured another shot of whiskey, drank
it, and then threw the empty glass across the room. It crashed
against a wall, and the noise snapped him out of his trance.

He placed the open bottle back in its hidden compartment under the shelf, and, as he turned to go, he heard the sound of footsteps on the wooden plank walk outside. Suddenly the saloon door
swung open.

The man in the doorway was a stranger to Dave. Small beads
of sweat ran down a tobacco-stained gray beard not thick enough
to hide the ugly scar running across his cheek. He held a revolver, and before Dave could say a word, he fired it.

If Dave had been in front of the bar, he would have been dead.
Instead, the bullet hit the wood, showering splinters in all directions. Dave drew and fired automatically, and his bullet didn't
miss. It smashed into the left side of the stranger's chest and
spun him out of the doorway, where he took two stumbling steps,
fell off the boardwalk, and landed facedown in the dusty street.

Dave leaped over the bar and rushed out the door—then dove
for the street as a second shooter fired at him from across the
street. Dave blasted off two quick, wild shots that missed hitting
the man.

The man raced to a horse tied outside the pharmacy, mounted,
and galloped away.

Dave leaped up and ran to the middle of the street. Using both
hands, he took careful aim and fired. The rider screamed, lurched
over on his horse, yet managed to hold on and soon disappeared
around the bank building.

Dave frowned grimly. He knew he had hit the second mysterious assailant, yet he had no wish to follow him or to finish him off. He walked over to the stranger he'd killed and looked at him without pity. He thought for a moment of burying the man but quickly shook his head. That was not his worry. He reloaded his Adams quickly and slid it back into its holster. He pulled three large splinters from the bar from his arm and threw them to the street, scowling at the blood dripping off him.

He went to the bearded man's horse, stripped off the saddle and bridle, and let it go free. It saddened him to think he had more compassion for the horse than for the man he'd just killed. The horse stood quietly in the middle of the street, seeming uncertain of what to do. Dave clucked to the horse, and it started slowly down the street.

Dave walked back to the newspaper office, mounted Chocolate, and growled in anger, "Old girl, I hope Betty can tell me what happened here, 'cause I sure as hell can't."

As he rode out of town, bitterness mixed with sadness inside him, and he sighed. This wasn't the homecoming he had planned.

Chapter Two

Dave rode to Betty's house deep in thought; too many questions, too many things he couldn't believe were happening. Where were all the people of Quiet Valley? Where was his father? Most perplexing of all, why should two strange men ride into town and try to kill him without warning? The war was over. So what was that all about? He shook his head, trying to think clearly, but he came up with no answers.

Perhaps he should have gone to Betty's first, but he'd been a little afraid to. He hadn't written much and not at all while working as a spy in the South. She'd said that she'd wait for him, but four years was a long time for a beautiful woman to wait. Perhaps too long.

As he approached her house, he suddenly felt a burning excitement inside him, the same joy at just being near her that he'd had when he came to take her to their first dance.

He rode up to the gate and gazed at the yard in shocked disbelief. It never occurred to him that she might also have vanished. The yard was knee-high in sunburned weeds. Dave always remembered the small two-story house as the prettiest home in the valley, but today it looked pale and drab, with a sinister appearance that caused his stomach to churn.

He eased off Chocolate and pushed the gate open. He pulled his Adams and moved watchfully up to the house, keeping his eyes on the windows. How many times in the last four years had he approached a building, not knowing what awaited him? How many times before had he felt the comfort of his Adams in his palm and the fear knotting his stomach? He had hoped to forget those memories.

6

Cautiously he opened the unlocked door and eased in silently. He wanted to call out, to hear Betty's cheerful reply, but he didn't.

He made a quick tour of the four rooms downstairs. There was nothing out of order, only dust covering dust. As he started up the stairs, he heard a noise. He froze instantly and listened. From somewhere upstairs came a faint squeaking sound.

He strained to hear which room the sound came from. Was he at war again, where the lucky lived, and the unlucky died? Or perhaps it was the lucky ones who died. He pressed himself against the wall and placed his feet gently on the outer edge of the stairs to minimize any creaking of the steps. The cold sweat that formed on his face was an old, unwelcome friend.

Suddenly his foot hit a loose board, producing a squeak. Dave froze again and waited. His hands were clammy, and a slight tremor ran through him. The silence settled like a thick fog. He wanted to run up the stairs, firing at anything that moved. He sucked in a deep breath and slowly exhaled, forcing himself to calm down. The last four years he had survived by not overreacting but by staying calm and using his head. After another long, slow breath, he started up the stairs again.

By the time he reached the top landing, he'd fixed the noise as coming from the front bedroom. The squeaking sound occurred irregularly; it would start and then stop for a few moments.

Dave moved silently to the closed bedroom door. With one ferocious kick from the heel of his right boot, he smashed open the door and fell into a low crouch. The crash of the door echoed throughout the house like a thunderclap, but no gunfire followed.

Betty's mother lay in the bed. When he took a few steps inside, the smell told him he was too late.

Unexpectedly, he heard the squeak again, behind him from the left. He spun in that direction, but he didn't shoot. He slammed his free hand against his mouth. His body started shaking, and he couldn't stop it. Betty, his lovely Betty, sat in a rocking chair, rocking with the movement of the wind through the open window in her rocking-chair grave. She had been dead a long, long time.

Dave ran out of the room to the head of the stairs, gagged twice, and fought against the pain he felt. He had seen death before. Men killed by the horror of war. Yet that was part of war, and you learned to deal with it. The people were mostly strangers, and in time you became hard and calloused to death. But this wasn't a battlefield. This was home, and the women in that room were no strangers. He slid the Adams back into the holster and wiped away the tears running down his face with the back of his hand.

He stumbled down the stairs, his body still shaking. There were old copies of *The Quiet Valley Weekly* in the front room, and he rolled them into a cone. He lit the paper torch, smashed the oil lamps on the walls, and pushed his torch into the oil. He watched with tortured eyes as the rooms roared into savage flames.

When he walked out of the house, streaks of fire crawled up to the second floor, burning brightly with loud, crackling noises. Chocolate strained against her reins and snorted loudly at the flames. She calmed down when Dave spoke to her and patted her gently. He took his canteen, swished a quick swig around his mouth, and spit the ugly taste of bile to the ground. He leaned his head against the saddle and closed his eyes. After a few moments, he mounted Chocolate.

He rode again toward Quiet Valley in the evening dusk, not looking back at the fire lighting the sky. He rode with empty eyes and an empty heart. There was no need for questions, no need for answers, no need for life, no need for death, no need for anything. He headed Chocolate over to a dark grove of pine trees by the side of the road. In the cool solitude he sat in the dirt and buried his head in his arms.

Moments later he heard the sound of horses coming down the road. He glanced up to see a group of ten or more riders heading for the burning house at a hard gallop. They carried their guns low and looked too hard to be miners or farmers. They had the same look as the scar-faced man Dave had killed earlier. The riders reminded Dave of the guerrilla bands he had ridden with on occasion in the war. Was it possible that this band of hard men had taken over the valley? Even so, if that were true, what had happened to the people? Had this mob killed them all? Surely not. But who or what had killed Betty and her mother? Dave stood, his pain replaced with a growing, seething anger.

The dust from the riders settled slowly back to the road. He mounted Chocolate and circled back to Betty's house. He kept his distance and tied Chocolate away from the house, then silently crept up to where he could see the riders in a tight semicircle in front of the burning building.

A tall, scrawny man appeared to be the leader. He wore a loose-fitting black broadcloth frock coat and vest. The flames silhouetted his homely face. It looked as if nature had forgotten to place flesh between his bones and his skin. A black Vandyke beard failed to cover up his thin lips or weak chin. A thin black cigar, held tightly in his teeth, glowed brightly as he issued his commands. His low, hollow voice seemed to come from deep within the man and caused Dave to shiver slightly when he heard it.

Dave returned to Chocolate and quietly moved away from the blaze. He would spend the night in his old childhood hideout. One thing he knew for sure, he intended to remain in Quiet Valley. He'd come home for peace and found another war. So be it. He knew a lot about war.

He allowed the horse to set her own pace as he headed back toward the mountains. There would be no dozing in the saddle tonight, no matter how tired he was. The moonlight let him make out the trail with some ease, but the shadows it created all looked like hidden dangers.

When he stopped to let Chocolate rest, the sweet pine smell surrounding him almost made it seem as though this ugly day hadn't happened. He stepped out of the saddle and stretched stiffly. The memory of Betty and her mother filled him with pain. He shook his head, hoping to dislodge the memory, knowing he couldn't.

He heard a horse snort and the gruff laughter of a man. He quickly pulled his Adams but realized the laugh was twenty yards or so up the trail from him. He moved silently through the underbrush in that direction. Peering around an old stump, he saw a young man lying on the ground with a rope tied under his armpits, his hands bound behind him. It looked as though the older man on the horse had been dragging him.

Although the young man gasped in short, pained puffs, he made no other sound. Dave soon discovered why. The old man pulled out his knife and, with a laugh, squatted in front of the young man. "You knows, kid, since you can't talk anyways, I reckon I should just cuts your tongue out. How'd you like that, huh?"

He started to laugh again, but it turned into a hoarse, hacking cough. He straightened up, spit tobacco juice onto the ground, and stared down at his prisoner. "Kid, I knows how I's gonna git you walking faster. I tie this rope around your neck. Then when youse falls down and I pulls you, I don't gotta listen to all them damn grunting noises." He started laughing at his cleverness as he pulled the rope from under the young man's arms and placed it around his neck.

Dave watched the scene with mixed emotions. He'd learned in the war not to become involved in anything that wouldn't help him, yet he knew there was only one thing his conscience would accept—saving the young man.

The old man adjusted the rope into a slipknot and pulled it tightly against his captive's throat. Dave knew he couldn't risk shooting the old man. There could be others close by. There was only one quiet way for the old man to die, and that was by a knife. But Dave was too far away to sneak up on him, so he'd have to throw it.

His bowie knife was not good for throwing. The last time he'd tried to use it that way, it had gone end over end. Rather than the blade hitting the man, the handle had hit his head and knocked him out. Dave had been lucky that time, but the incident still embarrassed him whenever he thought about it. He sighed silently. There was no choice; he'd just have to chance it again.

Dave pulled out his knife and rose to a crouch. He waited until the old man straightened up with his back to him. With a smooth, overhand motion, he hurled the knife. This time his throw was perfect, and the blade sank deeply into the man's back with a low, deadly thud. The old man gasped and stumbled. He tried to pull his gun, but fell facedown on the ground and didn't move.

Dave stood in the shadows with his Adams out and ready, looking for others. The young man on the ground strained to see what had happened.

The horse, smelling the blood of its dead owner, bolted and

raced down the trail. Dave listened to the sound of the retreating animal and cursed softly. Then he came out of the shadows. He placed one foot on the back of the dead man's waist, leaned over, and pulled the knife out from between his shoulder blades. The slight sucking noise repulsed him. He wiped the knife clean on the man's pants, then cut the rawhide binding the young man's hands.

Once free, the youth quickly pulled the rope from around his neck and gasped in deep breaths. Dave helped him to his feet. Even in the moonlight, the boy's cut and swollen wrists made Dave wince. He was younger than Dave had thought, perhaps seventeen or eighteen. His clothes were tattered and bloody.

Dave whispered, "Was he the only one?"

The boy nodded.

"Good. You'd better come with me until we've had a chance to talk."

He nodded slowly.

"Can you ride?"

He nodded again.

"Come on, then. We've a ways to go before we're safe."

Dave helped the boy climb into the saddle, then climbed on behind him. Chocolate was tired and complained at the extra load, swishing her tail at the aggravation, and it took another hour before Dave reached his long-ago hideout. He dismounted and led Chocolate up a dry creek bed that looked as if it ran straight into a large granite cliff but actually veered off to the right. He approached a fortress of pine trees and shrubs and after some moments found what he was looking for, a large cave entrance hidden behind the trees.

He led Chocolate into the cave, coaxing her forward with gentle whispers and soft clucking, but she moved reluctantly into the dark, strange place. The boy remained slumped in the saddle in a pained, exhausted sleep. Dave left him there and hurried back outside to use some pine branches to smooth out any visible hoofprints on the ground leading away from the rocky creek bed.

Once back inside the cave, he took Chocolate's bridle and groped his way blindly forward. He wanted to light a candle but decided not to risk it. After twisting back and forth almost twenty feet through the winding cavern, Dave spotted the entrance to a small valley.

The valley formed a small triangular hollow about fifty feet deep, with the high point where they were emerging. There were cliffs on all sides, which made it an excellent place to hide. Of course, it could also turn into a deadly trap.

He glanced around, and a hint of a smile crossed his face. Long ago he'd built a small log cabin and lean-to stable in the hollow, and even in the darkness, he could see they still stood.

He waited just inside the cave mouth, checking for any activity. Although he didn't see anything, he felt edgy. Finally he led Chocolate out of the cave with the boy still asleep in the saddle. Unexpectedly, he tripped on a rope stretched across his path. He caught himself before he fell, but the trap released a bucket of rocks that went crashing down the small slope. Dave instantly reined Chocolate back into the cave and drew his Adams.

Awakened, the boy sat up straight, a puzzled look on his face. Dave waited. He could hear his own heartbeat echoing against the walls of the cave.

He tried to force the panic from his mind. He needed to think clearly. He realized that he was in a bad spot. He placed an ear against the cold stones of the cave and listened for any vibrations or noise that would tell him someone was moving in after them. There was only silence and his own heavy breathing. Still, the only reason for a setup like that trip wire would be to set off an alarm. Or to kill him. He turned and gently helped the young man off the horse, then noiselessly stripped the saddle off Chocolate. He threw one leg over the back of the horse but hung low on the far side, his Adams in his hand. He hoped the person or persons inside the cabin would think only a wild horse had wandered in.

Chocolate moved slowly with uncertainty and some whinnying. Just when he neared the cabin, he heard a noise behind him. He craned his neck and saw the young man walk directly to the cabin. Before he could overcome his amazement, the boy stepped inside.

Dave slipped off Chocolate, crouched, and swung his Adams in a semicircle, trying to see into the rock piles on either side of the cabin, expecting shots at any moment. Just as he cautiously stepped inside the door, the young man lit a small candle.

Dave took one look at the candle and yelled, "Damnation! Blow out that damn candle 'fore you get us both killed."

The boy, however, was writing something on a piece of paper. He then held out the note. Dave hurriedly read it. *I set that trap.*

"Hell you did! When?" Dave exclaimed.

The man took the paper back and wrote on it. *Two days ago.*

"How in the hell did you ever find this . . . no, on second thought, why'd you ever leave it?"

He wrote, *No food, two days.*

"Ah!" Dave exclaimed. He looked at the tired and bloody young man in front of him and wondered what had happened. Whatever his story, he knew it wouldn't be a happy one. He sighed. "Good reason." He patted his stomach and announced, "Hell, that's what we both need. Some grub to perk us up."

Dave went back to the cave, set the trap rope again, and carried his saddle to the stable. Chocolate followed him in, and he quickly took care of her needs. He glanced around one last time, nodded, smiled slightly, and carried his saddlebag back to the cabin.

A fire was out of the question. The smoke and cooking smell could travel too far. For tonight, it would be a cold supper. Dave laid out what food he had, and the two men ate silently as the candle cast eerie shadows around the cabin.

He'd built bunk beds in one corner, and the table they were eating at was an old crate with two carved logs as seats. The cabin was still in good shape, even with no repairs since he'd left— better than many places he'd stayed at in the South.

A potbellied stove stood in a corner. Five years ago, Dave loved to tell close friends how it took him two days of sweat and backbreaking labor to haul it up to his private hideout. Now, he had no desire to tell stories. Now he simply wanted answers to his own questions.

After they finished eating, Dave lit an old, battered pipe and leaned back against a wall. "Guess we'd better introduce ourselves. My name's David Kramer—Dave."

The man wrote on his scrap of paper, *Ted Jones.*

Jeff R. Spalsbury

Dave nodded, "All right, Mr. Jones, how about filling me in on what's been going on around here?"

Ted went to the bottom bunk. He unrolled a blanket, lifted a new rifle, and placed it against the wall. He removed an envelope from the wrap and handed it to Dave.

Ted started to sit again, but Dave looked up at his taut, tired face and said, "Why don't you go on to bed? I'll read this, and then we can talk about it in the morning. Take the bottom bunk."

Ted nodded his thanks and laid the blanket out. He stretched out on the bed and was asleep immediately.

Dave removed the papers from the envelope. Slowly reading the letter in the flickering candlelight, he hoped it would have answers to his many questions. When he finished, he placed the papers on the table, relit his pipe, and stared over at Ted. According to the letter, Ted's father had made a contract to transport fifty Sharps rifles and ammunition to the Army fort near Livermore, but a wrong turn had his dangerous cargo veer into Quiet Valley by mistake.

A man named Jedd Scott had discovered what Ted and his father had in the wagon and attempted to kill them for it. Ted had narrowly escaped. Scott's men had tracked him up into the mountains. Almost discovered, he dove into the bushes in front of the cave and discovered Dave's long-ago hideout. Then hunger forced him out to look for food.

From Ted's description, this Jedd Scott was the same skeleton of a man Dave had seen at Betty's house. It was a good name for the man. *The Undertaker,* Dave thought to himself.

The writing in the letter showed that Ted Jones was well educated, but Dave now realized that the young man knew even less about what had happened to the people of Quiet Valley than he did.

He walked out of the cabin to check on Chocolate and inspect the trap again. Then he went back inside, pulled off his boots, and climbed into the top bunk. He, too, was asleep immediately.

Chapter Three

At first light, Ted woke and stared out the cabin door at the valley's granite walls. Though exhausted, he had not slept well. His entire body ached, and the memory of his father's death kept exploding in his mind. He wanted to pull the blanket over his head and escape from the world, but he eased painfully out of his bottom bunk and limped out to the small spring. His wrists still hurt from his bindings. He dropped his arms slowly into the coldness of the water and let it numb some of the pain. He splashed the cold water onto his face and felt the stinging from all his cuts and abrasions. He gently patted his puffy and swollen left eye; at least he could still see out of it.

Tall and lean with wild, light blond hair and soft blue eyes, Ted knew he looked younger than his nineteen years. He dried his wrists gently on his shirt, ran a hand through his hair, and walked back to the cabin.

As he started in, he stepped on a small twig, and it broke. Dave Kramer flung himself out of the top bunk with his Adams in his hand.

Ted jerked back against the door and crumpled to the dirt floor. Dave squeezed his eyes open and shut a few times, trying to force himself fully awake. Then he grinned sheepishly at Ted when he realized what had happened. "Well," he said, as he scratched his head with the barrel of the gun, "that's one way to get me up quickly."

He flipped the Adams back onto the bunk, jumped down, and held out a hand to Ted. Ted gulped nervously as Dave pulled him back up.

"Sorry," Dave apologized. He gave the youth a gentle slap on the back, then sat on the bottom bunk and pulled on his boots. He strapped on his gun belt and smoothly slipped the Adams back into the holster. He walked out to the spring and tried to untangle some of his mess of brown hair and wash up. When he returned to the cabin, Ted had laid out what little food they had left for breakfast. Each ate quietly and, when finished, Ted wrote, *What are you going to do with me?*

Dave picked his teeth with a small twig, stopped, and said evenly, "Well, you are something of a problem. You have family anywhere?"

Ted slowly moved his head back and forth.

"Nobody?" Dave replied in surprise.

Again, Ted indicated no one.

"Huh," Dave mumbled. "You're your own man, then. If you'd like, I can lead you out the back pass to Livermore."

Ted shrugged his shoulders and wrote, *I—no money, no nothing.*

Dave nodded silently.

What about you? Ted wrote.

Dave looked across the table at him. "I was your age when I went off to war. I thought it would be something special. But war isn't special. It's ugly and dirty. I saw more death than a man should see in a hundred lifetimes. I spent most of the war working alone. . . ."

While he explained to Ted what his role in the war was like, he tried to decide what to do with the likable young man. He saw the innocence in Ted he'd once had himself, and he had learned in the last four years to trust his instincts.

Ted listened to Dave's tale intently. He wrote, *I'm sorry.*

"The last few days have been hard on both of us," Dave said slowly. He stood and leaned against the doorway. "I must be honest with you. I don't know what to tell you to do."

Ted stared into his half-empty cup for a long time, and then he wrote, *May I ride with you? I have my own debt to pay.*

Dave read the note with Ted's request, and his forehead wrinkled while he pondered the question. He felt responsible for the youth, yet could he ask him to stay here and fight, to kill, maybe to die? During the last two years of the war, he had worked behind enemy lines as a spy, discovering important information that others hadn't been able to learn.

Jamie Blackfoot had taught him how to survive. Helped him to survive. But Jamie was a professional. Ted Jones was far from that. Ted was a greenhorn.

Dave smiled to himself. Yes, Ted was about as much of a greenhorn as he was when Jamie took him on. Ted had his reasons for wanting to stay here, and his reasons were just as valid as Dave's. He frowned and looked away. It was so much responsibility, another person's life. He stared out the door.

Ted watched him closely. Then Dave let out a long sigh and with a shake of his head said, "You know if you stay, there's a good chance you could get killed?"

Ted nodded.

"You'll likely have to kill men yourself." Dave looked at him sternly. "You'll have to take orders from me and ask no questions. What do you have to say to that?"

Ted nodded that he understood.

Dave picked up his cup and gulped down the last of the spring water. "If you don't have any more sense than that, I reckon we'd better get some food up here and find you a horse."

Ted agreed with a nod and a smile of relief.

Dave motioned to the rifle in the corner and asked, "Where'd you get the Henry?"

Ted wrote, *A gift from my father.*

"The Undertaker didn't get it?"

Ted looked puzzled.

"Sorry, that's my name for the man you called Jedd Scott."

Ted nodded thoughtfully, apparently agreeing with the choice of a name.

"Sharps rifles, right? That's what you said in your letter." Ted bobbed his head.

"Got any ammo?"

Ted shook his head.

Dave picked up his saddlebag and pulled out a box of shells. He tossed the box to Ted.

Ted looked at the shells in amazement.

"I've got a Henry too. Figured I'd have trouble finding cartridges, so I bought quite a few. Was going to use it as a hunting rifle." Dave didn't smile at the irony of his words.

Ted laid his rifle across his lap and deftly pushed in the bullets.

"How good are you with it?"

Ted wrote slowly, *I demonstrated rifles for my father. He said I was the best shooter he'd ever seen.*

"You were close to your father, huh?"

Ted looked down at the rifle and nodded slowly.

"Yeah, I was to my father too. I know how you feel," Dave said softly. "Let's go get you a horse."

It took longer to get back to the town of Quiet Valley than Dave had expected. Chocolate had to carry the two of them, and even though she was going downhill, she was still tired from the long ride yesterday. And in case Jedd Scott had his men out looking for them, the trip required extra caution to be certain they weren't seen.

At a small ridge overlooking the town, Dave came to a stop. He slowly scanned all the buildings. Ted motioned to Dave, but Dave had already seen the guard on the roof of the bank-hotel.

The two-story building was an ideal spot for a sentry. The man could see the center of town and the road into it all from the same location. While a good spot, it would only work if the sentry was not taking a nap. And from what Dave could tell, the guard was asleep in his chair, his rifle leaning against the rail.

"I'll need to take him out," Dave said calmly.

Ted removed a scrap of paper and a stubby pencil from his vest pocket and wrote quickly. He handed the note to Dave. The note said, *Doesn't it bother you to kill someone?*

Dave tried to find the words to answer him. "That's a tough question to answer," he said thoughtfully. "For the last four years, I've done nothing but kill and see killing. You try not to get calloused, but . . ." He paused, then shrugged. "What can you do?" It wasn't much of an answer, and he knew it.

Dave dismounted and briefed Ted on what he wanted him to do. Ted nodded that he understood.

It took ten minutes for Dave to work his way to the bank-hotel. He wasn't as worried about the sentry on the roof as he was that the whole thing might be a trap. Perhaps there was more than one guard.

A ladder went from the ground up to the stable roof and a second ladder from the stable roof up to the top of the bank-hotel. Why hadn't the guard pulled up that second ladder? Too lazy? Dave knew his thinking wasn't as sharp as it should be, but that second ladder made him nervous. He felt the muscles in his jaw tighten. His instincts were warning him.

He stopped and looked around carefully again. He stood silently, trying to spot a problem, making sure he hadn't missed an obvious hint of trouble, but nothing stirred, and all appeared normal except for that damn second ladder. He knew he had two choices: go back and figure out another way, or go ahead with his plan. He continued to stand silently, pondering his options, still scanning the area for any sign of a trap.

Finally he made his decision and moved cautiously to the stable. The single horse inside the stable ignored him. He climbed the ladder silently to the roof. Moving noiselessly across the roof, he climbed the second ladder until his head just reached the edge of the second roof. He peered over warily. The guard hadn't moved. Dave reached for his bowie knife, when he heard a loud click behind him. He twisted his head and looked down into the big barrel of a Sharps rifle. The man holding it motioned him back down. Dave eased slowly down the ladder and dropped his gun belt and knife on the stable roof as the man ordered.

The man laughed roughly and motioned with his head to the sentry. "That's just a dummy."

"Damnation," Dave mumbled.

The man laughed again.

Dave looked at him and hoped Ted Jones was as good a shot as he claimed. Or would he shoot? He'd likely never killed before, and now, for the first time, when he had to, would he? Dave sighed softly.

Dave figured the man had climbed onto the stable roof right behind him. He noticed that the man was wearing moccasins. Very clever. That's why Dave hadn't heard him.

Ted could have shot him at any time, unless he was waiting for the sentry on the roof to make a move. If that were the case, Dave wondered how long it would be before Ted realized the roof guard was only a mannequin.

The gunman motioned Dave to the edge of the stable roof and told him to jump down to the street. Dave jumped off and landed on all fours. He stood, turned, dusted off his hands, and looked up at the man. If Ted didn't fire soon, it wasn't going to matter how good a shot he was.

The guard started to laugh but never finished. Almost in unison, the guard grabbed his chest, and the rifle report echoed throughout the town. Dave took a deep breath. That was close. Too close.

The man's rifle dropped and went off harmlessly against a corner of the bank building. A moment later, the man rolled off the roof and crashed to the street.

Dave motioned wildly for Ted to get Chocolate and ride down to him. He climbed rapidly up to retrieve his knife and gun belt. He jumped back off the roof to the street as Ted rode up.

Ted stared at the body of the man he'd just killed, and Dave could tell from Ted's white face what guts it had taken for him to pull the trigger.

"Are you all right?" he asked.

Ted nodded weakly.

"I know it's hard. I was sick for three days after I killed my first man."

He hurried into the stable, grabbed the gunman's horse, tightened the saddle, and mounted quickly, telling Ted to follow him on Chocolate.

Ted motioned to Dave to leave town quickly, but Dave said firmly, "No," and motioned with his hand. "Come on. Here's where you'll have to trust me."

Riding swiftly around the bank-hotel, Dave led Ted past another group of buildings before he stopped behind the last one. He jumped down, opened the door, and told Ted to take Chocolate inside. He led the captured horse in after them and closed the door behind him. He handed the reins to Ted.

"Put the horses in that bedroom," he said, as he motioned to a room on the left. He grabbed his Henry and hurried into the front office.

Dave was in the building he knew better than all the rest, his home and the office of *The Quiet Valley Weekly.* He pulled a stool to the front window, where he could see down the street. Ted returned a few moments later. Dave pulled out his pipe and filled it with tobacco.

What about tracks? Ted wrote.

"We're okay," Dave said, while he lit his pipe. "That sentry on the roof faked us both out, huh?"

Ted nodded. His body went as limp as the mannequin's.

"Yeah, but I was the real dummy," Dave admitted.

Ted disagreed and motioned he'd realized it almost too late.

"No, that was a dumb mistake on my part. My instincts were telling me it was all wrong, and I didn't listen. Thanks to you, I'm still ticking. Thanks for saving my bacon."

Ted nodded and solemnly studied the Henry he held in his hands.

"I was mighty serious when I told you what we're up against. You may have to use that rifle again. If you want to get out now, I'll understand."

Ted shook his head determinedly.

"There's nothing pleasant about killing. I know."

They remained silent for a long moment. Then they heard the thunder of horses galloping up the street, hard and fast, like an approaching storm. Dave took a quick look and saw Jedd Scott and four of his men ride by.

Ted motioned to Dave that Scott might have his men search the town.

"I'm betting they don't. When they don't see our horses, I'm hoping they think we took off once we shot the guard. Sometimes you've got to play the odds, even when they're not in your favor. Anyway, I figure we're safer trying to make a fight of it here than we would be out in the open.

"You go on back and keep the horses quiet. Watch out the back window. If you see anyone, give two taps on the buttstock of your Henry. Don't just start blasting away."

Ted nodded and hurried silently toward the bedroom.

Dave snuffed out his pipe and put it away. The heat inside the building was intense, and his shirt was soaking wet, the sweat running down his arms. He cocked the Henry and placed it beside him.

It grew quiet again, and Dave strained his ears. But aside from the occasional shuffling of the horses in the back room, the silence settled around him like a thick fog. It descended on him like the heat and felt more deadly than death.

Dave found himself mesmerized by a fly buzzing around a spiderweb in a corner of the windowpane. Dave wondered if he were the spider or the fly. The spider was not in sight, yet Dave knew it must be close by. Suddenly the fly landed on the web. It buzzed excitedly as one leg and then another became caught in the spider's trap.

The spider appeared from nowhere and watched, as if in silent satisfaction, while the fly's buzzing became as intense as a scream of anguish. Exhausted, its movements slowed by the grip of the web, the fly stopped struggling. The spider moved rapidly over the web for the kill. No more anguish, no more joy. One lives, the other dies—the law of the insect world, the law of war, and now, evidently, the law of Quiet Valley.

Just as the drama in miniature ended, Scott and his gunmen rode away into the distance. Dave got up guardedly by the side of the dusty window and watched to make sure it wasn't another ruse.

The mannequin was still on top of the bank-hotel. Dave called back quietly to Ted that he was going out. He moved swiftly out the front door and ran to the general store. To his surprise, the door opened, and foodstuffs remained on the shelves.

He quickly filled three dusty grain sacks. When he checked the gun shelf, it was empty, as he'd expected. He hurried back to the newspaper office.

Dave saw Ted still watching out back, although periodically glancing through to the front. Ted was going to be all right.

Dave studied the desks. His former desk by the window was covered with old clippings of newspapers and letters, and the front-page form was locked tightly and ready to be moved to the press. He blew the dust off and read the reversed type quickly. He could do that since he was twelve.

Cholera!

Well, he finally knew what had killed Betty and her mother— and why nobody had wanted to touch the food. Fear. He glanced at the three grain sacks and pursed his lips in thought. A doctor once told him that you couldn't catch cholera from food unless it had been handled by someone with dirty hands. It was bad water that caused and spread cholera. He hoped that was correct, because he and Ted needed this food.

Could cholera have killed everyone in town? He'd heard of such things happening, but if that were true, wouldn't there be more dead bodies of the townspeople about? And how did Jedd Scott fit into all this? Dave still had too many questions and not enough answers.

He sighed softly and hurried back to where Ted stood guard. The youth no longer looked as pale as before.

Dave asked, "Hot enough for you?"

Sweat soaked Ted's shirt and vest. He wiped his forehead and threw the sweat at Dave.

Dave grinned and said, "I agree. How does it look?"

Ted motioned with his hand. *All clear.*

"I know you'd like to get some water, but I just found out that there was cholera here. For now we are going to have to tough it out from my canteen. But I never heard of a horse getting cholera, so we'll give them some from the well."

The water from the old well behind the building pumped out cold and fresh, and the horses drank deeply. Dave handed Ted his canteen, and they each took a long swig. Heading back to the hideout, Dave took a different route, along the far side of the valley.

Abruptly, he reined to a halt.

Ted looked at Dave, puzzled.

Dave pointed down at a farmhouse, and Ted saw smoke drifting lazily upward into the midafternoon sky.

Dave twisted around in his saddle and asked, "You ever hear where Scott was holed up?"

Ted bent his head in thought and then wrote, *Bowman.*

"Yes." Dave nodded. "That would be a good spot at that. The old Bowman Fort. When I was growing up, we just called it The Fort. It's a big adobe building, Spanish style, with two stories and a stockade fence running around the whole place. Ezekias Bowman built it long after the last of any Indian problems; nobody ever knew why." He paused as he thought about it some more. "It would be a tough place to attack. Easy to defend. Yup, for the Undertaker, it would make sense. Have you any idea how many riders he has?"

Ted wrote, *Saw ten, but way he talked, there could be more.*

"Well, he's lost three in the last two days. I think we've gotten his attention, no matter how many he has."

Ted reached over and jerked Dave's sleeve.

"Yeah?"

Ted shrugged and pointed at the farm, asking whose place it was.

Dave studied the small farm below them. "Not sure. Mayor Peterson's family used to live there, but they were old. They didn't have any kids, and there's a woman with a baby in the yard. And a few cows and chickens." Dave paused and studied the area.

"What's peculiar is I only see one old, swaybacked nag. How could anyone run a farm without more horses?" He frowned, puzzled. "And if it isn't the Peterson place anymore, whose place is it? Why has Jedd Scott left them alone?"

Ted softly tapped his rifle stock and pointed to a man who sat against a tree away from the house, a rifle beside him.

"Yes, well, isn't that interesting? I wonder if he's meant to keep people in or us out." Dave smiled grimly. "You know, this was a right friendly valley when I left. Perhaps we should go down and pay a social call."

Ted scribbled a note and handed it to Dave. *Chicken dinner?* was all it said, but from the gleam in Ted's eyes, the implication was plain enough.

Dave slowly scratched his four-day beard and smiled. It had been a long time since he'd had a chicken dinner.

As they rode down into the valley, Dave wondered if this particular spider might not get quite the meal it intended.

Chapter Four

Dave and Ted headed slowly through thick brush to the valley floor. They halted behind a dense thicket that totally hid them from the road and the farmhouse. Dave tied the horses and whispered directions into Ted's ear. Ted nodded that he understood.

Dave had to cross an open field, so he crawled part of the way and soon was behind the guard leaning on the tree. When he drew closer, he saw that the guard was reading a book, his rifle nearby on the ground.

Pretty careless, Dave thought. *You don't leave a rifle in the dirt.* Not until he was within a few feet of the guard did he realize that he wasn't a man but a woman in pants, shirt, and a beat-up, flat-brimmed hat. It shocked him. Even in the worst of times in the South, he'd never seen a woman in trousers.

He crawled silently up to the tree the woman leaned against. She was so absorbed in the book, she had no idea he was there. Dave eased his Adams out and reached the barrel around the tree until it was mere inches from her head. He pulled the hammer back.

The sound of the gun cocking caused the woman to suck in her breath and freeze. Her head moved around until she stared right into the barrel of the Adams. She raised her eyes to his.

They were huge brown eyes that reminded him of the eyes of a frightened baby fawn. She must have been seventeen or so, for while she had a youthful cuteness about her, she also had the mark of a woman. Even the drab clothes couldn't disguise the curvature of her body.

He reached over, grabbed her collar, and jerked her to her feet, still holding his gun on her.

Dave noticed that her knuckles were turning white from clasping her book so hard.

"The Bible?" Dave asked.

She answered in a low, sarcastic voice. "Yes, the Bible. Maybe you ought to read it sometime, if you even know how to read."

"Do you recall the Psalms?"

She gazed at him, puzzled.

"The one that goes like this: 'The Lord is my light and my salvation; whom shall I fear? The Lord is the strength of my life; of whom shall I be afraid?' Behave yourself, and you'll be all right."

He motioned her to the path leading up to the farmhouse. When they got closer, an older woman saw them, grabbed the baby, and raced back into the house.

The girl asked, "Do you plan to rob us and kill us?"

Dave jerked back on her collar so angrily, he almost pulled her out of her boots. "Now you listen to me, girl, and listen well," Dave hissed violently into her ear. "I've been through hell these past two days, and I'm in no mood for a sharp tongue."

He shoved her ahead of him. When they got to the front of the house, a large man came out carrying an ancient, smooth-bore shotgun.

"Your father?" Dave asked.

She nodded silently.

Her father was a huge man with hairy arms and a bushy black walruslike mustache. He wore no hat and except for a small ring of black hair running around his head, he was bald.

He spoke harshly. "Sir, if you have hurt my daughter in any way, by God, I'll break you in two with my bare hands."

Dave started to reply, when he glimpsed a movement by the side of the house. At the same time, he heard a tapping sound and watched the father's eyes move from Dave to Ted's hidden location.

Dave said firmly, "My friend is a very good shot. Tell whoever is by the side of the house to move out into the open with you."

The father motioned with one large arm, and Dave saw the

girl's mother. She carried an old flintlock that looked as though it could hurt the person firing it more than whomever she aimed at.

"Now," Dave said, "if you will please put down your guns."

For a moment, he felt that the father was going to try something foolish, but the man slowly placed the shotgun on the ground. His wife also laid the flintlock down.

At that moment Dave realized that the girl's father was already a defeated man. His shoulders slumped, and he turned from a solid rock to a bit of runny clay.

Dave shook his head in amazement. This man who, a few moments ago, had looked so strong and alive had changed before his eyes into an old, beaten creature. The bluff for his daughter had failed, and, with that failure, he'd lost all his strength and courage.

Dave asked, "What name do you go by?"

The father paused, puzzled, but finally said, "Byrne. Ralph Byrne. You should know that already."

"Why should I know that?" Dave questioned.

"Why should you know?" the girl retorted sarcastically. "You work for Jedd Scott, and he told all his gunmen not to touch us. He'll kill you for this."

"What if I told you that I don't work for this Scott fellow?"

"I'd say you were lying."

"Spunky little critter, aren't you?" Dave glanced down at the girl and asked, "What happened to the Peterson family?"

Mrs. Byrne looked at her husband and asked, "Pray, how'd he know who used to live here?"

Mr. Byrne hushed her with a glance and gave Dave a long look. "What is your name, sir?"

"Dave Kramer."

"A Kramer used to run the newspaper," Ralph Byrne replied softly.

"My father. Do you know what happened to him?"

Mr. Byrne shook his head. "I've heard of him, that's all."

"From whom?" Dave asked.

"You want to know the answers to many questions." He didn't wait for a reply, but added, "But you've come to the wrong place. I can't help you." He paused again and added in a low voice,

"I can't help anyone." Mr. Byrne shook his head. "Please don't shoot my family."

Dave released Julie's collar, uncocked the hammer of his gun, and smoothly dropped it back into the holster. "I wouldn't hurt them, sir."

Julie straightened her shirt, then turned and stared at him with both relief and anger. Before she could speak, Ted ran from his hiding place, pointed up the road with his Henry, and flashed a fist and two fingers.

"Scott?"

Ted nodded.

Mr. Byrne's face turned pale. "That must be Jedd with his men. You have to leave!"

"No time," Dave muttered. "Everybody into the house. Byrne, get the shotgun and flintlock." Once inside Dave asked, "D'you want to fight them off?"

"Oh, no! No!" Mr. Byrne exclaimed. "Hide in the back. Julie, take these men to your room."

Dave stared at him for a long moment. Sweat poured from Byrne's face, and his cheek muscles were twitching rapidly. The man was terrified.

Julie motioned Dave and Ted into her bedroom and whispered for Ted to slide under her bed. Dave looked around and noticed a small doorway covered with a cotton drape. A small storage space, but it had enough room, even with the trunks and boxes, for him to squeeze in.

Julie sat on the edge of her bed and started twisting and un-twisting a corner of her shirt, her fear as apparent as her father's. It was as if she knew something bad was going to happen and yet was praying it wouldn't.

Dave heard footsteps come down the hall. He slowly slid his Adams out. Maybe, he thought, Ralph Byrne had told Scott about Ted and him.

Julie's stiff body showed her fear. The door opened. Julie's gasp told him what he already knew; they were in a tight spot.

Jedd Scott's voice boomed out in his eerie way. "How say you,

Julie? I wondered why you didn't come out to greet me. That's not very hospitable of you, is it?"

Dave could see through a split in the cloth door. Mr. Byrne stood in the doorway behind Scott. Sweat ran profusely down his face, and his gaze darted around the room, looking for them.

Dave suddenly realized that the Undertaker wasn't after them; he wanted Julie. Scott seemed happy to see her, but from Julie's clenched fists held stiffly at her sides, she was clearly terrified.

Scott gave a loud laugh and said, "Well, let's see if you still love me."

"Please, Jedd," Mr. Byrne implored, "leave her be!"

Jedd spun and screamed, "Shut up! Shut up!" He yelled at his men, "Watch him! Keep him out of here!" Then he slammed the door in Byrne's face and turned back to Julie. "Now, Julie . . ."

Dave watched in amazement as Scott grabbed her and pulled her to him. "You know, Julie," he murmured in a low and evil way, "I sometimes wonder if I shouldn't have taken you rather than your sister, Henrietta." He started kissing her roughly as she squirmed, helpless in his grasp.

Julie's back was to Dave, so he couldn't see her face, but from the whiteness of her hands, Dave knew she was going through hell. His mind slipped back to the war.

He'd been told to go to an old and almost totally destroyed Southern home. He needed to meet a Union officer there, and he had information needed by General Rosecrans.

There were three horses outside, but no one was on guard, which made Dave wary. He heard what he thought was a woman's scream when he rode up, but then the house was quiet. He slipped around back and crawled through a destroyed window opening. Once inside, he again heard the hysterical scream of a woman. He moved quickly through the deserted room and peeked through a small crack in a door to see a Union lieutenant and his two men taunting a young girl. She was tied to a chair, the lieutenant's pistol aimed at her head. She screamed as he pulled the trigger, but the only sound was a dull click as the hammer struck an empty chamber. The girl's parents lay dead across the room. "Now just tell us where your parents hide their gold, or the next time this won't be empty." He waved his pistol in front of her face.

The girl was totally out of her mind and incapable of answering. She shook her head wildly back and forth.

Dave never questioned what came over him. He just kicked opened the door and started firing. The next thing he remembered was someone shaking him and telling him to stop. His soul felt trapped in the middle of a nightmare. He had killed all three of the Union ruffians. Two Southern soldiers had shaken him back to his senses. They had seen him enter the house and followed him in. He'd been firing time and time again at the three dead men.

The Southerners were part of a unit trying to cut into the Union's supply line. His killing the three Union men convinced them he was one of them and allowed him to infiltrate the group and destroy their plans. But the memory of that horrible scene had etched itself on his mind and still woke him in a cold sweat late at night. He had no remorse for the three men, only for the young girl who a week later had hanged herself.

If Julie hadn't been standing in his line of sight, Dave knew he would have shot Scott right then and there.

Scott stopped manhandling Julie, turned, and walked out the door, laughing softly while Julie stood whimpering like a wounded animal.

Dave closed his eyes and fairly shook with fury. As he slowly controlled the burning anger in himself, he heard a commotion as Ted crawled out from under the bed, also in a rage. Dave grabbed him before he raced through the door.

Ted spun on him angrily and motioned to the gun Dave still held in his hand.

Dave understood but he grabbed Ted by the shoulders and said firmly, "Ted, I know how you feel, but what about the rest of this family? We kill Scott now, and his men open fire. Everyone dies, including us." Dave stared at him hard. "Do you understand?"

Ted reluctantly nodded.

Julie sat down on the bed, showing no emotion. She stared at the wall, not crying, not whimpering, just stone-faced.

Dave went to her, bent down on one knee in front of her, and asked softly, "Julie, has this happened before?"

Her eyes were glassy, and she didn't reply. He looked at her chalky face. He had seen the same look on new recruits after their first battle. Dave's stomach twisted inside with pity for this gentle girl.

Mr. Byrne burst into the room, and Ted almost fired on him before he recognized the man. He looked at his daughter, tried to speak, couldn't, then turned sorrowfully and walked back out. His wife came in with tears in her eyes, took her daughter into her arms, and gently held her.

Dave asked harshly, "What madness is—" He was so angry, he lost his voice for a moment. He slowly regained control over himself. "Why in the hell don't you fight this bastard?"

The mother shook her head.

"Where is Henrietta?" Dave demanded.

Again she gave no answer. Dave looked down at the crying woman holding a daughter who appeared all but dead inside.

He stormed out of the bedroom, with Ted close behind. Ralph Byrne sat in a rocking chair, his arms crossed in front of him, his hands tucked under his armpits. He cried softly, his eyes staring at the floor as he slowly rocked back and forth.

Dave gaped at this huge tower of a man, unable to protect his family from the Undertaker and his minions. He sighed heavily, motioned to Ted, and shook his head. "Let's go. There're no answers and nothing we can do here."

They returned to where they had hidden the horses, climbed into the saddle, turned their horses away from the Byrnes' farm, and headed for their hideout.

Chapter Five

Dave and Ted rode silently, each man deep in thought. Abruptly, Dave pulled Chocolate to a halt and said decisively, "Ted, I think we ought to go up to the old Bowman Fort and find out what the hell we're up against. Are you all right with that?"

Ted nodded silently. He pointed to their bags of supplies.

Dave nodded. "Always thinking of food?"

Ted wagged an index finger at him, and Dave smiled for the first time since they'd left the Byrnes' farmhouse. "Yeah, I know. I thought we might have a chicken dinner tonight, but we'll just have to put up with another cold meal. We'll stop here, eat, rest, and then head for the fort after dark."

After eating, they stretched out under the pine trees. Dave watched the sun go down with mixed feelings. He'd almost forgotten the beauty of the sunsets in the mountains, yet now he wondered if this might be his last. Through the war he'd forced thoughts of his own mortality out of his mind; now they kept resurfacing, like an omen, and he didn't like omens.

Dusk played with shadows against the mountains as they started back down into the valley, but after only fifteen minutes of riding, it turned burned-cork dark. The cool, dry air felt good after the heat of the day. A moonless night exploded the stars, which shone clear and bright across the sky. Dave felt as though he could reach up and touch them from his saddle.

He had been to the Bowman Fort many times. Such a strange and unusual place, it stood out clearly in his memory even after all these years. Dave explained to Ted that Ezekias Bowman had planned to build a great ranch. He started by erecting the huge log cabin on a high ridge overlooking his land. Then came the barns, the bunkhouse, and to top it off, a huge stockade-type log fence around the entire place. Unfortunately, Ezekias wasn't as good at raising cattle as he was at building things. All that was left of the Bowman ranch now was the fortress on top of the ridge. Zeka, Ezekias' son, had sold off most of the cattle land to start the bank in town.

Ezekias had died long before Dave was born, and as far as Dave could recall, Zeka had never kept the place up. Two years before Dave left for the war, a barn caught fire one morning when a hired hand, still drunk from the night before, knocked a lantern into the hay. The barn turned into a flaming inferno, the smoke visible throughout the valley. Everyone who saw it came to help, and though they couldn't save the barn, it turned into the biggest social gathering of the year.

Zeka, a grizzled old bachelor now, lived in town and ran the bank. Dave could remember many a night when Zeka, Dr. Zimms, Mayor Peterson, and his father had sat in the back of the *Weekly* office arguing over nothing while drinking beer and playing poker.

Dave heard Ted gasp when they rode up from the creek bed and saw the silhouette of the fortress against the starlit sky. Lights flickered behind the stockade posts, and they saw two guards walking back and forth at the top.

"The Undertaker doesn't take any chances, does he?" Dave whispered, laughing softly at Ted's wide eyes. Dave knew the danger this evening presented. Not only was it going to be a problem getting into the Bowman Fort, but getting back out could be even more difficult.

Dave outlined his impromptu reconnaisance plan to Ted and arranged where to meet afterward. Then he dismounted and handed Chocolate's reins to Ted. With a quick nod, he cautiously started weaving his way from bushes to trees, up the slope to the stockade wall.

At the far end, the two guards on the wall smoked and whispered quietly. When he reached the wall, he moved stealthily away from them. He heard the mumbling of their voices slowly fade.

He felt along the massive fence for the roughest log he could find to try to shimmy up the wall that was at least twelve feet high. The two guards chatting not over thirty feet away greatly lowered his chance of success.

He took off his hat, pushed his hair back, and frowned. Then he continued stepping away from the guards, feeling each log. When he came to the corner of the fence, he stopped. With a slight shrug, he turned the corner and kept working his way along the wall.

He took only a few steps when he stopped abruptly again. He wanted to laugh aloud. Scott, apparently not satisfied with some of the logs in the wall, had started to replace them. His men hadn't quite finished, however, so they'd leaned the last three logs against the top crossbar, leaving a gap in the fence.

Dave hesitated. Maybe it wasn't as funny as he thought. He'd been set up once today; he wasn't eager for a repeat. He cautiously felt around the inverted logs for some type of trap. There didn't seem to be any.

He sighed tiredly. Perhaps a trap, perhaps not. Either way, he decided, he was going through. He took out his bowie knife and, using it as a probe, slowly snaked his way through the opening. Once inside, he knelt and took a deep, silent breath. It wasn't a trap. That carelessness surprised him. And the high weeds inside the stockade hid him easily.

The back of the big house stood directly in front of him. He could make out light from the front of the house but none shone from the rear.

He half crept, half ran to the nearest window. Jedd Scott's distorted voice boomed from the front part of the house, but Dave couldn't make out what he was saying. He tried the back door and windows, but everything was locked. At least high growth around the house made it safe for him to crawl toward the front.

He crouched under a window with light shining out of it and heard Scott shouting, "I don't care what you think! If you're not man enough, I can always get Hutton to do it."

"It ain't that. It's just that we'd be giving ourselves a lot of extra trouble if we don't keep it all Northerners. We start mixing them, and there's sure to be trouble."

"I tell you, when I get through, Hilary, they won't think of North or South anymore. They'll just think of me. I'll be the king of this whole Territory, not just this damn puny valley."

"Sure," the voice replied, but with no conviction.

"Listen," Scott said reassuringly. "I got word that ten of Bishop's men are riding in to join us. With them, we'll have enough to strike Fort Livermore."

"We can't do that without more ammo. We're too damn low to attack Livermore, even with more men."

"You worry too much. We'll get the new wagons. And with what we've already got, we'll be in fine shape. You've got a guard on it, don't you?"

"Sure, Jedd. You ain't still worried about that boy, are you?"

"Worried? Hell, no. Why should I be worried?" Scott's voice turned frenzied. "You dumb bastard, in the last two days he's killed three of our men, and we still don't know where he is. Hell, he could be outside this window right now, for all you know!"

Dave swallowed quickly and hoped no one would check that out. He heard Scott stomping around the room; then the voice full of sarcasm and contempt boomed out again. "Why, Hilary, I think I might even like the boy. He's the only one around here who's matched my intelligence or guts!"

Dave heard someone walk up onto the porch. He slowly eased his way to the rear of the house again. So Ted was being blamed for all Scott's troubles. That would make the boy grin. Scott's outlaws were getting low on ammo. Now, that was valuable information. If he could destroy their existing ammo and get the regulars from Fort Livermore, they could squeeze this pus out of Quiet Valley.

He hurried around to the other side of the house and looked over at a bunkhouse that still stood. From the lights and activity there, he knew it would be some time before the men bedded down.

He tried to think of where the outlaws would store their ammunition. He squatted in the high grass and tried to remember the last time he had walked around the Bowman Fort. Suddenly, he remembered a dugout, a double-walled icehouse near the entrance. That would be a perfect spot to store ammo. But to get there, he'd have to go to the front of the house, then move down the road in full view of the bunkhouse, the house, and the guards on the stockade. The man talking to Scott—Hilary—had mentioned a guard on the ammo. Was that in addition to the guards on the stockade?

He maneuvered around the house and scanned the open space in front of him. The tall grass and dried weeds in back of the house had given him adequate cover, but up front the ground cover had been flattened or totally worn away. The path was flooded with light from the bunkhouse and main house. Even if he tried to crawl to the icehouse, the guards on the stockade would see him.

One other option occurred to him, but he frowned as he pondered it. He could simply walk down the path as though he belonged to the group. Sweat formed on his palms as he thought about it, and he quickly wiped his hands on his trousers. Hell of a place to be if he got caught.

Two men sat on a crude bench outside the bunkhouse. While Dave watched them, one flipped his cigarette out in front of him and said something indistinguishable to the other man. They stood and went inside.

Dave looked around cautiously. If they caught him out in the open . . . He shook that dark thought from his mind. He looked around once more, took a deep breath, and walked toward the road.

He tried to look as casual as he could. The two guards on the stockade were talking, and from where they stood, they wouldn't be able to see the door into the dugout. He tried to stare into the shadows of the icehouse but couldn't see another guard. As he made his approach, he slowly exhaled but just as quickly sucked his breath back in. There was a man sitting in a chair, leaning back against the icehouse door.

The man stood quickly and pointed a shotgun at him. "Who the hell are you?"

Dave said nonchalantly, "Bishop. I just got in. Hilary says I'm supposed to relieve you."

"It's about time." He held out the shotgun and spit tobacco juice off to one side.

"Put it by the chair."

"Sure." He turned and placed the shotgun against the chair. Before he could turn back around, Dave shoved his bowie knife deep into the guard's back. Blood flowed over his hand when he pulled the knife back out. He gulped a breath of air to keep from vomiting. He hated using a knife.

The guard's body fell back against him, and he guided it into the chair. When he finished, it looked as though the guard had simply fallen asleep. Dave placed the shotgun in his lap.

The door wasn't locked, but a crossbar kept it closed. Dave lifted the bar off and slipped in, pulling the door closed behind him. He felt in his pocket for his match case and soon had a phosphorus match lit. He saw two candles on a shelf, lit one, and shoved the other into his shirt pocket. The icehouses in Quiet Valley were usually double-walled structures half-buried in the ground. Dave felt sure the light wouldn't be seen from the outside. Even so, he quickly glanced at the walls to make sure they were intact.

This icehouse was big, almost twenty feet long and about eight feet wide. No ice remained in the room that now held many wooden boxes. He could tell at a glance that some of the crates contained rifles. Moving back, he saw black powder and cartridges. "Wow," he said in a shocked whisper. He berated himself for speaking out loud. *If this is what they call being low on ammo,* he thought, *being well-stocked must mean a huge arsenal.*

He moved over to one box off by itself and lifted his candle to read the label. PATENT BLASTING OIL. He gasped aloud again. His eyebrows shot up. He wasn't about to touch that stuff—a mixture of gunpowder and nitroglycerin, the most dangerous explosive known to man. He'd seen it used twice during the war. He carefully backed away from it.

A wooden keg of black powder sat open, the lid loosely on top. From it he poured a pile of powder onto the floor and in lines leading to the other kegs. Then he placed the first keg on its side so the remaining powder would flash up inside and set off the others. He took the other candle, cut it shorter, lit it, and ever so delicately placed it in the center of the pile of powder. A delayed fuse, the candle would burn down until it touched off the black powder leading to the full kegs.

Dave looked at his bomb approvingly, calculating that it would go off in about ten minutes. He started to go out the door, when he heard someone walk up to the guard outside.

Before he could leap out and silence whoever it was, the man gave a loud yell.

He was in big trouble. He glanced back at the candle and the small pool of wax forming at its base. He stared at it for a long moment and then nodded, deciding on another long shot.

He grabbed the other candle and, working rapidly, melted it as quickly as he could into the pile of powder, all the while hearing more men hurriedly approach. He crawled over the kegs and rifle boxes and slid down behind them just as the door flew open.

Not sure if they had seen him or not, he held his breath and tried not to move even a muscle.

The men came in quickly with lanterns and guns drawn. They all saw the candle at the same time. A baldheaded man with a week-old beard quickly fell to his knees, gently lifted the candle off the powder, and snuffed it out.

"That kid's like a ghost!"

Scott's voice boomed out. "Where is the little bastard?"

"From the amount of wax melted, looks like he's got about a five-minute start on us," a voice replied.

Others crowded into the icehouse. Jedd Scott's voice, filled with frustration, yelled, "I'll give a hundred dollars in gold to the first man who brings me that boy's body!"

They looked around at one another. Money was a form of loyalty they all understood.

The door of the icehouse slammed shut. Dave slowly took a deep breath. The blackness of the dugout was like a prisoner-of-war cell.

He shivered. Sweat ran down his face. He wiped his forehead with a shirtsleeve, shook his head, and tried to remain calm.

Sliding over the crates, he felt with his hands as he worked his way back to the door. He pressed his ear against the wood and listened. Finally, satisfied that no one stood guard outside, he pushed against the door. The crossbar was back in place.

He felt a keg by the door and sat down on it in despair. "Damnation," he mumbled softly.

Chapter Six

Dave wanted to light the candle he'd shoved into his shirt pocket, but he didn't, knowing he might need it later. The door was the only way out. Somehow he had to figure out a way to lift the crossbar off. It had been a long day, and, from the look of things, it was going to be an even longer night.

Then he heard someone coming.

He pressed his ear against the wood door and heard the footsteps approaching. He slid his Adams out and prepared himself. With no light, he knew he couldn't hide behind the kegs in time. He only hoped that whoever it was would come inside.

He heard the bar being lifted off its hooks. He took a deep breath and waited for the door to open. He felt his heart pounding. His eyes strained to see the door open.

But it didn't open.

After a long moment, Dave exhaled. Had they discovered that he was inside? Did they want him to break free, so they could shoot him on open ground? That way, they wouldn't take a chance of blowing up their ammunition cache. Dave knew only too well how dangerous the blasting oil was. He was sure Scott's men knew that as well. One errant bullet, and they could all be blown up.

Or maybe someone had started to come in and changed his mind. But why wouldn't he put the bar back?

Dave flicked a bead of sweat from his eyebrow. He cautiously reached out with his left hand until it touched the door. He carefully pushed the door open a few inches. The night air rushed in, and Dave enjoyed its cooling sensation. He waited, but nothing happened. He pushed the door again so he could stick his head out. He looked up at the log cabin and the bunkhouse. There were a few lights on, but otherwise all was quiet. Too quiet, in fact.

He pulled the door shut again. *Well, if they're waiting outside to give me a present, maybe I should leave* them *one*. He pulled the candle from his shirt pocket and lit it. It was short, but he figured it should burn almost five minutes before igniting the powder.

He stepped out of the icehouse, and the cool night air chilled his sweaty body. He looked around cautiously. If they were getting ready to ambush him, they were well hidden. He glanced over the edge of the icehouse's sod roof at the stockade. He saw no guards.

The only thing that might save him was if Scott's men still thought it was only Ted Jones causing all the trouble. They knew what Ted looked like, but they didn't know what *he* looked like.

He gulped in a deep breath and started walking up the road to the main house. If they were baiting a trap for him, this path would be the place. He had his Adams in his hand and walked slowly but steadily toward the cabin. Off in the distance, he saw a few men checking out the remaining buildings on the property, but no one paid him any attention.

When he neared the house, he saw the glow of a cigar tip from the porch and almost shot at it, when a hollow voice rang out, "Well, did you see any sign of him?"

There was no mistaking that voice, and for a moment Dave wanted to shoot Scott and be damned. But he knew it would be instant suicide. Obviously, Scott thought he was one of his own men.

Dave called back, "No, thought I'd check around in back, just in case he tried to circle around."

"Ha! No chance of that. Now he's just hoping he can get out of this valley alive."

Dave walked around toward the back of the house and, when he was out of sight, broke into a quick trot up to the fence. He slid out through the gap and hurried down the ridge.

He was in the shadow of the trees, at the bottom of the ridge, when his bomb went off. The huge roar lit the night sky with flames, followed by a glowing cloud of white smoke.

If Scott's men hadn't spotted Ted, he should be waiting about a quarter of a mile from the fort, by Lonely Creek, under a small overhang. Dave hurried to the spot and saw the horses hidden in a grove, but no Ted.

Something was wrong. He tensed, his hand on his Adams. But before he could make a move, a soft Scottish voice whispered to him from nearby, "Now don't you be making any crazy moves, Davey my boy, or I'll dump your wee friend in the creek."

Dave relaxed as the memory of that voice came back to him. "I once knew a hard-drinking Scotsman with a voice as gravelly as yours."

"Gravelly as mine?" the voice exclaimed indignantly. "Sure'n I've got a voice that many a lassie has wept over."

Dave hurried to the man standing in the shadows, and they shook hands heartily. It was Jamie Blackfoot, his wartime mentor and close friend.

Jamie had the smell of someone who hadn't bathed in weeks. His long, tangled red hair flowed over his shoulders. Dave could never decide whether Jamie was more Scotsman or Indian. He had the humor and coloring of the Scots and the toughness of an Indian. He was short, usually dirty, and probably the best friend and teacher Dave had ever had while he was in the war.

"That was a mighty loud bang back there, Davey."

"Well, you know, someone just opened up the fort's icehouse door for me, and since that was so nice, I figured I'd better finish my business there. You wouldn't happen to know who let me out, would you?"

"Well, someone had to light a shuck for that poor soul trapped in there. Course, I never expected it to be you."

"I thought so. Thanks. That was a bit of a tight spot I was in. Now, where exactly is my young friend?"

"You mean that wee young mountain cat *is* your friend?" Jamie exclaimed. He pointed into the shadows of the overhang.

Ted lay there, gagged, his hands and feet tied. Dave hurriedly cut his bindings loose. When he was free, Ted tried to explain things to Dave. Dave interrupted him while he helped him to his feet. "Don't feel bad, Ted. This is Jamie Blackfoot. He taught me all I know about warring, so if anyone had to best you, know you've been bested by the best."

Ted shook Jamie's hand sheepishly.

"Aye, he's a wee bit of a devil, isn't he, Davey?"

Dave smiled and nodded. "He tries pretty hard."

They quieted as two horses galloped down a trail close by, heading for the Bowman Fort.

As the sound of hoofbeats disappeared into the distance, Dave asked Jamie, "What the hell is going on around here?"

Jamie looked at Dave in surprise. "Why, laddie, ain't the Army sent you here to help me?"

Dave shook his head emphatically. "This is my home, or at least it used to be. Ted Jones here is the son of the man who brought the rifles intended for Fort Livermore into the valley by mistake."

"Aye." Jamie shook his head. "That was a bad affair. T'weren't nothing I could do about it."

Jamie squatted on his haunches, pulled out a tobacco twist, and, after some struggling, bit off a chunk and started chewing it with great effort.

Dave squatted with Jamie. Dave knew this ritual well; they had done it many times in the past. Ted remained standing to keep watch.

Jamie spit once and said to Dave, "I heard you were dead."

"Guess I'm a hard man to kill. For that matter, I heard the same thing about you a piece back."

Jamie spit again into a nearby bush, grunted at Dave's remark, and nodded toward Ted. "He don't say much."

"He can't."

"Well, for a tadpole, he fights like an Indian buck."

Dave glanced up, and Ted flashed a smile. Praise from Dave's teacher was not to be taken lightly.

"So, what the devil's going on around here?" Dave asked.

Jamie nodded. "Jedd Scott and his men stole fifty thousand

dollars of government gold. The Army transferred me here to work on it with the Wells Fargo men."

"Why Wells Fargo?" Dave asked.

"Scott stole it off a stagecoach. It seems the Army and Wells Fargo are downright sentimental about fifty thousand dollars. So they sent me to infiltrate Scott's gang right after they took over this valley—"

"How'd they take the valley?" Dave interrupted.

"Why, don't you know, laddie? The plague, cholera, or something nasty—whatever it was damn near killed off just about everybody here. Those who didn't die left in a mighty rush. I heard tell it was a great panic. There were a few folks left, but Scott took them prisoner up at the fort." Jamie chuckled. "He's not a very trusting man."

Dave nodded. "I can believe that."

"I tell you, laddie, whatever it was that killed the people scared the hell out of me and the other men, but I guess it'd run its course by the time we came in."

A look of hope crept into Dave's face. "Jamie, you wouldn't know if my father is in there, would you? Bob Kramer?"

"Laddie, all I sees is the doctor and the other outlaws. Scott keeps us away from the prisoners. I'm not sure how many there are, but Scott's got the women cooking for us, and the men take care of the horses and such. I see them once in a while but never to talk to them." Jamie paused for a moment and then added, "Of course, there's the Byrne family—they still live in the valley. Do some farming for the fort. Something mighty strange going on there."

"I can believe that. Ted and I had a little run-in with that family." Dave told Jamie what had happened.

"Aye," Jamie said slowly. "One daughter, Henrietta, helps out the women during the day in the kitchen. I've heard that Scott locks her up at night with a leg iron. We hear her crying in the wee hours. It's a mournful sound."

Ted pulled on Dave's sleeve and pointed toward the fort. They heard a commotion and lots of yelling.

Dave said, "You'd better get back before you're missed, Jamie."

Jamie stood and eyed the fort with disgust. "Davey, there's two things you can kindly do for me."

"Ask."

"Well, laddie, I don't want Scott's scalp lifted until we've figured out where the gold is."

Dave nodded without pleasure.

"Second, I want you to meet with the Army and Wells Fargo men with me. Can you make it to Livermore by Saturday?"

"I can try. What day is it today?"

Jamie grinned at him. "Wednesday."

"Where?"

"At the Golden Spur. Anytime after eight."

Dave rubbed his growing beard. "A bath and a shave sound real good."

Jamie shook his head. "You always did smell too clean. Natural odor is better for your body."

Dave laughed and held out his hand. "Be careful."

Jamie took Dave's hand. "Aye, laddie." Jamie turned and shook Ted's hand. "You keep a close eye on Davey now."

Ted nodded.

Jamie turned and glided silently into the bushes, heading toward the fort.

Dave turned to Ted and said, "Quite a character, huh?"

Ted nodded quickly.

They mounted their horses and cautiously started onto the trail, when the sound of hoof beats and a woman's scream caused them to quickly pull back into the trees. Dave motioned for Ted to follow him, and they worked their way through the underbrush until they saw two men struggling with a woman on the road.

They quickly dismounted, and Dave motioned for Ted to remain on that side of the road while he crossed to the other.

The men were so busy trying to tie the woman's hands, they didn't even see Dave run across the road. The woman was on her stomach, and it was taking the best of both men to hold her down to tie her hands.

Dave yelled, "That's enough!"

Jeff R. Spalsbury

The men stopped and looked around.

"Who's that?" a man yelled back at him.

Dave decided to bluff. "Hilary. You know Scott doesn't allow you to mess with her."

They looked in the direction of Dave's voice, then quickly drew their guns and fired. But Dave had already moved. Ted and Dave fired in unison, and both shots hit their mark. The two gunmen fell on either side of the woman, and their horses bolted.

Dave ran out to the road and yelled at Julie Byrne, "Woman, what the hell are you doing out in the middle of the night by yourself?" He grabbed her by the arm and jerked her to her feet.

Dave knew that when the men at Bowman Fort heard the gunshots, they'd come riding. He yelled to Ted, "Get the horses!"

, Ted hurried to comply. When he gave Chocolate's reins to Dave, he mounted and told Julie in a tight voice, "Get up behind me, and be quick about it." He pulled her roughly up behind him, and they turned and dashed off.

They were no sooner concealed around a small bend when a group of horsemen raced up. One rider jumped down and checked the fallen men. "Both dead!" he yelled at the leader.

"Let's go get him, men. There's money on his hide."

Dave had counted on the outlaws stopping at the bodies, but he also knew that, riding double, they wouldn't be able to outrun their pursuers.

"Julie, ride with Ted." Dave motioned to a grove of trees some distance ahead and told Ted, "Hide there, and let them pass. Then take Julie up to the hideout. They think you're the one causing all this, so they should be satisfied when they only see me."

Ted tried to motion that he should do it, but Dave shook his head. "I know the country. You don't. If they see you, use your Henry, and I'll circle and try get them in a crossfire."

Dave gave Ted a wave and headed up the road again. He had three advantages. He knew the country, it was dark, and his horse was fresh.

Scott's posse came up behind him sooner than he expected. Dave figured there must be at least fifteen of them. He remembered there was a hundred-dollar reward for Ted's body, which, in this case, was *his* body. He spurred Chocolate into a dead run and raced toward the mountains. They were firing at him and coming way too close for easy living.

It was a gentle climb uphill for the next two miles. Chocolate seemed to sense that the bullets were meant for them and soon was running as smoothly as Dave had ever felt her go. He did not look back, but when the bullets stopped, he knew he had gained some distance from the outlaws.

The dark outlines of the first mountain crevices appeared, and he raced between two ridges. The riders were almost a half mile behind him but still too close for a quick turn-off.

His plan was to circle around them by going up a small canyon, then over a ridge to a canyon on the other side. His problem was trying to remember which canyon to turn into. One of them ended in a box of sheer vertical rock walls. It would be a one-way trap if he picked the wrong one.

He'd have to make a quick judgment and hope his call was right. The trail twisted through thick groves of lodgepole pines and aspen. He approached the first canyon and, after peering into the dark entrance, decided it was the next one he wanted. He remembered there were two big round boulders at the top of the ridge in the dead-end canyon. But when he slowed up to look, his hunters picked up on him. He let Chocolate have her head, and soon they came to the second canyon. He turned Chocolate down into the dim trail.

It was dark and rough going, and he could tell from the way Chocolate snorted and felt along the path that she didn't like it. He couldn't see his pursuers, although he could hear them. The canyon had steep walls. He looked up at them—and saw what he didn't want to see. Outlined at the top against the starlit sky were two large round boulders. He had picked the wrong canyon!

There was no use going on to the end. He jumped off and led Chocolate forty feet off the trail, then listened to the riders' horses going slowly by. The men cussed when their mounts slipped and whinnied.

Dave suspected that they would leave a guard at the entrance. He figured right, for he heard one man whisper as they passed, "This really a dead end?"

"Damn right. We got that rabbit now. We'll post guards every fifty feet. He'll be flushed out and damn soon."

Dave smiled grimly. He'd really done it this time. He waited until the last of the hunters moved past. Then he took four cloth boots from his saddlebag and fitted one onto each of Chocolate's hooves. Chocolate had been trained during the war to wear them and offered no resistance.

Since he'd stopped when he'd realized his mistake, he hoped he might be able to get by the guard at the entrance. The rest of the men would be farther into the canyon. He led Chocolate on foot back toward the entrance. When he saw two guards on their horses, he tied Chocolate to a small aspen tree.

He pulled his Henry and crept back down the trail. He could make out what he thought were three, maybe four, men spread out down the path. If he could bounce a shot off the canyon wall, it would ricochet, and they would never know what direction it had been fired from. He aimed for a rocky wall and pulled off one shot. That was all it took. In the next few moments shots were being fired in all directions. He scrambled back to Chocolate. The two guards galloped down the trail, firing at every flash of gunfire.

Dave untied Chocolate, eased into the saddle, and trotted out through the unguarded entrance. He had his Adams ready, but it wasn't needed. No one was there.

He didn't remove Chocolate's boots until he was far from the canyon. Even then, he still heard the sound of an occasional gun-shot reverberating. It was a long time before all the shots stopped, and by then he was far from that part of the valley.

It took him another hour to get up to the hideout. He heard two light taps when he approached the grove of pines in front of the cave. "It's all right, Ted. It's me."

He climbed down wearily. Ted took Chocolate's reins, his face full of concern.

"I'm all right, just tired," Dave explained. "This has been one long day, huh?"

Ted nodded.

Dave saw the tension in Ted's face and wondered how much of that was caused by his having to kill two men today. Dave found it hard to believe that so much had happened in just one day.

He sighed. Maybe he was getting old. He had no feelings for the men he'd killed today, and that bothered him.

Once inside their hideout, Ted helped him pull the saddle and gear off Chocolate, and Dave fed the horse. He left the stable open so Chocolate, along with Ted's horse, could move about the small valley for grass and water.

Julie was still awake. Ted had built a tiny fire in the stove and made some coffee. Julie handed Dave a cup, and he sat down and slowly sipped it. It was the first hot coffee he'd had in days. It tasted good. He looked up at Julie and said, "You had yourself in a bad way."

Julie nodded. "I was going to the Bowman Fort to see if Henrietta was all right, but there were men everywhere. They even fired at me till they saw who I was. Then they tried to kidnap me."

"They shot at you because they thought you were Ted here. They think there's just one of us."

Ted looked at Dave in surprise.

"Yeah, that's right," Dave said. "You, my fine lad, are the sole source of all the Undertaker's problems these last few days. I, on the other hand, am nobody. In fact, I don't even exist." He smirked at Ted.

Ted beamed, and Dave gave a small, short snort.

Julie said, "You didn't have to shout at me."

Dave spoke to her softly. "You're probably right. But when men are trying to kill me, I don't much worry about my manners."

She started to reply, but Dave stopped her with a wave of his hand. "You sleep in here. Ted and I will sleep by the stable." He stood stiffly, grabbed a blanket and his saddlebag, and went outside. He mentioned to Ted to check the trap by the entrance. "Make sure the horses can't wander out too."

Ted nodded.

Dave trudged tiredly to the spring and tried to wash up. The cold water felt painful, but he was glad to be cleaner.

Chocolate came to the spring and took a drink. Dave reached out and rubbed her nose. "You were good tonight, old girl." Chocolate gave a snort and returned to grazing on the grass around the cabin.

Dave spread open his blanket on the ground, laid down on one half, and pulled the other half over him. He was asleep immediately.

Chapter Seven

Dave woke disoriented and groped clumsily for his Adams. He relaxed when he saw Julie Byrne coming out of the cabin with the water bucket.

He'd slept till near noon, he figured wearily. He kicked the blanket off his legs and stretched. His beard was getting itchy. He ran his palm over it, then rubbed it roughly.

Julie was filling the bucket with water from the spring. He looked around for Ted but decided he must be in the cabin.

He picked up the blanket and folded it, then walked to the spring. "Here, let me see if I can manage that bucket."

She frowned at him and asked, "What are you going to do with me?"

Dave smiled gently at her. "If there is any way we can get you back home safely, we'll do it."

She nodded but didn't look convinced. Dave picked up the bucket and followed her into the cabin. Ted sat at the table, holding his head in the palms of his hands with his elbows propped on the tabletop. He was still half asleep. Dave took a cup, dipped it into the cold spring water, and poured it on top of Ted's head. Ted sprang to his feet with a surprised grunt. His boots were still on the floor, and he grabbed one and threw it at Dave. Dave ducked the boot and laughed at Ted. "That will teach you to look half awake at noon."

Ted scribbled on a piece of paper, *No way to treat your bodyguard!*

"Bodyguard!" Dave roared. "Why, you young snip." Dave

grabbed the youth in an armlock and said laughingly, "What I have to put up with."

Ted playfully poked his elbow into Dave's stomach.

Dave let go and held up his hands defensively. "I give. Any man who would hit me in my empty stomach is too mean for me."

Julie watched from the doorway, smiling shyly at them. Dave glanced out the window and said to Ted, "You know, I think we can have us a little fire. The wind is in our favor, so the smoke should be all right. How about a hot breakfast?"

Ted grinned his approval.

"You go and find me some dry wood, and I'll see if I can get a little blaze going." Dave opened the stove door.

Ted grabbed a long twig from the wood box and gave Dave a swat on the rear as he hurried out the door. Dave yelled, "Hey, now, you bushwhacking devil!"

Ted flashed him a triumphant smile from outside the door.

Julie spoke up. "What happened to Ted? I mean, why can't he talk?"

"Don't know," he said bluntly.

"Can't he talk at all?" she asked.

Dave shrugged, "Well, he can grunt some. I know a doctor from the war who helped people learn how to talk again. Figure I'll send Ted to him once we get this valley straightened out. Maybe he can help him."

She said hesitantly, "He's no kin of yours, is he?"

"Man doesn't help only his kin. He helps those he can help." Dave looked out the door at Ted coming back with an armload of twigs and branches. "Anyways, Ted's special."

Julie smiled at him and said, "You're not quite the person I thought you were."

"Now, what do you mean by that?" Dave demanded.

She looked at him smugly and said, "I thought you were just another outlaw, another killer, but I was wrong. You make a lot of noise, and the war has made you nasty tough on the outside, but I don't think you're that tough underneath."

That caught him off guard. He turned away from her and walked out the door.

Ted watched him go and then came into the cabin. He set the wood down and looked at Julie, puzzled.

She explained, "I guess I embarrassed him. I said he was nicer than he let on."

Ted smiled broadly at her.

"What's he really like?" she asked.

Ted pulled out a pencil and wrote on his tablet. *He saved my life. He's tough, but he's kind. He cares. He came home to Quiet Valley and found his father missing, his girl and her momma dead from cholera. It's rough to come home and find everything you love destroyed. He won't hurt you. He only wants to help.*

Julie read over Ted's shoulder. "Thanks. I believe you. It's been terrible for us all."

Dave walked to the edge of the spring, bent down, and splashed more cold water on his face. He stood and shook his head. Julie Byrne was about the most aggravating woman he'd ever met, yet something about her made him all tongue-tied. "Damn woman," he muttered to himself as he walked back to the cabin.

Julie did well with preparing the food Dave had found in town. The smell of beans, biscuits, molasses, and hot coffee filled the cabin. They ate quietly, although Ted would occasionally look at Dave, then at Julie, and laugh in his grunting fashion. Dave tried to kick him under the table but bumped Julie's foot instead, and that only embarrassed him more.

When they finished, Dave leaned back against the wall and said to Julie, "That was a mighty fine meal. We're obliged to you."

Ted nodded his agreement.

"Thank you." Julie frowned and asked, "You were at Jedd Scott's fort, weren't you?

"Yup."

"Did you see Henrietta?"

Dave shook his head. "But I heard about her."

"Tell me."

"It's not good."

Her mouth formed a tight line, but she nodded for him to go ahead.

Dave related what Jamie had told him.

Julie gasped, sprang from the table, and ran to the window.

Dave said earnestly, "I'm sorry, Julie."

He motioned for Ted to get the horses saddled, then walked up behind her. "I want to take you home and see what your father can do. It's about time he was able to fight back."

Tears ran down her cheeks, and Dave saw the despair on her face. "What can he do? Oh, I just knew that Jedd was hurting Henrietta. He's . . ."

Dave put his arms around her, and suddenly she turned and sobbed against his shoulder. When she stopped crying, she looked up at him. He kissed her gently on the forehead and said, "I hate to take you back home, but I can't see any other way."

"I know." She reached up, put her hand around his neck, and pulled his head down to her. This time she kissed him, and Dave felt the passion, the despair, and the loneliness inside her.

Ted came to the door and knocked lightly. Dave and Julie sheepishly looked at him, but Ted only made a low bow and, with a sweep of his wide-brimmed hat, motioned them to the horses.

Julie rode double with Dave, while Ted drifted behind them, keeping watch for trouble. They had to take their time, since Scott had his men out hunting for Ted. It was still a clumsy search in Dave's opinion, and he had no trouble in evading it.

They hid their horses in the same grove of trees they'd used previously. Ted slipped quietly up to the Byrnes' house to see if the coast was clear. He was back in a few moments and indicated that Scott and two of his men were there right now.

Dave's eyebrows drew together in a frown. That he hadn't figured on. If Scott discovered that Julie had been gone overnight, might he figure she was with them? He groaned and tapped his chin with his fist.

"What's the matter?" Julie asked anxiously.

"Scott might figure you were with us."

Ted grunted, correcting Dave by pointing to himself.

"Okay, with you." Dave glanced at Ted and added, "You think that's funny, don't you?"

Ted nodded.

"Yeah," Dave agreed with a quick grin, "it kind of is."

Ted made a "be still" movement with one hand and hurried back to where he could observe the farmhouse without being seen.

Dave motioned for Julie to stay where she was, and he went after Ted. Ted crouched behind a pile of rocks and weeds. He glanced around at Dave and then pointed to Scott and the two men riding away from the house. Dave stared at one man and gasped.

Ted jerked around and looked at him questioningly. Dave whispered in his ear. "See the shaggy-haired gunman riding beside Scott on the pinto? Notice how his face looks as if he's smiling all the time?"

Ted nodded.

"Well," Dave continued, "he's not. His mouth was slashed with a knife that formed a permanent scar. They nicknamed him Happy because of that scar. The problem is, Jamie Blackfoot was the man who knifed him."

Ted's face contorted in concern.

"Happy would just love to find Jamie and kill him. But if Happy just came in, maybe he hasn't seen Jamie yet. But if he sees Jamie first, Jamie's a dead man."

Ted nodded solemnly.

"I can't believe Happy's been here for long. Nothing would keep him from going after Jamie." Dave shook his head, then said, "We've got to get word to Jamie."

Ted nodded emphatically.

Dave squeezed Ted's shoulder. The youth was a rare find, Dave thought.

When Scott was out of sight, Dave hurried back to Julie. "If they know you were gone, you'll have to come with us. Let's go see your parents."

She looked up at him with her large brown eyes, took his hand, and said, "I'll do whatever you think is best."

Dave smiled down at her. Ted found a position by another boulder to check the road. He signaled them to go ahead.

Dave and Julie dashed to the big tree where they had first met. They crouched behind the tree, and he couldn't keep himself from smiling. Julie read his smile, pinched his arm, and scolded him, "Don't you laugh. You scared me silly, sneaking up on me like that."

He saw Ted wave for them to continue. Julie's parents must have seen them, for when they reached the door, it opened.

For one frenzied moment, Dave feared it was a trap. He shoved Julie behind him and drew his Adams so quickly, Julie didn't even see the draw.

Mr. Byrne filled the doorway, never knowing how close he came to stopping a .44 bullet. Dave sighed, quickly eased Mr. Byrne out of the way, and pulled Julie into the house behind him.

He glanced around the room to be sure it was safe. He stuck his head out the door, motioning to Ted that everything was all right in the house. Ted looked carefully around the area and gestured that he could see nothing.

Dave closed the door and watched Julie's mom and dad trying to hug and ask her questions all at the same time.

Dave said in a firm voice, "We don't have any time to waste. Answer my questions, and don't ask any until I'm done. Does Scott know that Julie was gone last night?"

"No, I don't think so," Julie's mother replied.

"Didn't he want to see her again, just now?"

"He asked about her," Mr. Byrne said, "but I told him she was sick. I thought sure he'd go into the bedroom to check, but he was really agitated about something. He kept chewing on his skinny stogie and ranting about killing a rabbit. I've never seen him like that."

Dave shook his head. "What about Julie's horse? What if he found it running free?"

"No, it came home last night all sweaty. We didn't know if she'd fallen off or what."

Mr. Byrne said to Julie, "We couldn't believe the note you left. Jedd would never let you see Henrietta, and if he had caught you up at the fort, he'd have kept you there too."

Dave interrupted before Julie could respond. "Why didn't you go out and try to find her?"

"We couldn't," Ralph Byrne explained quietly. "Two of Jedd's riders came and told us not to go outside or we'd be shot. Besides, the only horse Jedd lets us keep is that old plow nag Julie was riding."

"Well," Dave said, "we've been mighty lucky today."

Julie had her arm around her father and said, "You'd better sit down. You too, Mother. Mr. Kramer told me some distressing news about Henrietta."

She started to tell them but choked up. She stopped and asked Dave, "Please, can you tell them?"

Julie got Dave a cup of coffee as he told them what he'd already told Julie. Mrs. Byrne started to sob, and Mr. Byrne motioned Julie to take her mother to her bedroom.

Dave stared into his coffee cup. When the women had left, he said, "I'm sorry, I shouldn't have been so blunt."

Ralph Byrne shook his head. "No, we had to know. If only Jedd had never found us." He looked up as Julie came back into the room, holding the baby.

"I just don't know what to do," Byrne said, his voice filled with the pain of his family's situation. He looked up at Julie with tears in his eyes and added, "When I thought we had lost Julie too, I nearly drowned in sorrow." He stared at Julie for a long time. "You must take her with you. That's the only way she'll be safe."

"I can't leave you," Julie exclaimed, "or the baby."

Dave agreed. "She's right. If you had horses for everyone, I might try it. But even if we did, getting past all Scott's men would be almost impossible, particularly with a baby. My concern now is for Henrietta."

"But what can we do to help her?"

Dave looked at Ralph Byrne and said, "I'm afraid there's nothing you can do. But I . . . well, I can try."

"But how?" Mr. Byrne questioned. "You can't just go into Jedd's fort again and take her away."

A slight smile formed on Dave's face. "Matter of fact, that's precisely what I plan to do."

Julie's face turned pale. "Mr. Kramer," she pleaded, "you mustn't risk it. He'll be waiting for you. He'll kill you!"

Dave looked at her and smiled easily. "That doesn't seem like much fun. I'll try to avoid the being-killed part."

Julie looked nearly frantic. "You must not speak so lightly."

"Don't fret. I'll be exceptionally cautious."

"You must find a safer way."

Dave asked quietly, "Can you think of one?"

Julie shook her head. She was about to cry but trying hard not to.

"When we get Henrietta out, I'll take her to Fort Livermore and bring back troops. You'll know I've got her if Scott shows up here looking for her." Dave paused, and his face showed his concern. "You are going to have to act extremely upset about Henrietta's being kidnapped from the fort to keep Scott from taking Julie there."

"Surely he wouldn't try to . . ." Mr. Byrne didn't even finish his question.

Dave stood. "You'll have to bluff him. Otherwise, he'd probably kill you all. After he leaves, though, the four of you are going to have to get away from this house and hide out for at least a couple of days. Once I get back here with the troops, you'll know when it's safe."

He turned and started for the door but stopped and turned to Julie. "I'll need something to convince Henrietta I'm not one of Scott's men, that I'm there to help her. Have you anything I can show her or tell her?"

Julie frowned while she tried to think of something. Finally she looked down at her hands and said, "We have a family joke. Mother kids us when we say our evening prayers. She says, 'Make sure you say something in front of the *Amen*.' She'll know I'd never tell Mr. Scott that."

Dave nodded. He looked longingly at Julie. He hated to leave her there, and she read his thoughts. "I'll be fine, but my fear for you is great."

Dave nodded again and smiled gently at Julie. He turned, opened the door, and waved at Ted. Ted gestured all clear. Dave glanced over his shoulder at Mr. Byrne and said, "Try not to worry. I'll rescue your daughter."

He turned and hurried down the road.

Mr. Byrne turned to Julie and asked, "Do I sense a special feeling between you and this man?"

Julie watched Dave hurry down the path. "Some, Father. He's kind and sad, with a hard shell around him. He saved my life last night, and he'll probably rescue Henrietta, and . . ." She started to cry, and that caused the baby in her arms to start crying. Mr. Byrne put his arm around them both. "Oh, Father, if he gets killed, I'll just . . ." Her words drowned in her sobs.

"Don't cry," Mr. Byrne soothed. "He'll be fine." But when he said it, he knew it was only a wish.

Dave hurried to Ted and said, "The Undertaker doesn't know a thing about Julie's overnight absence. We'll go back to the fort tonight, get Henrietta Byrne out, and warn Jamie about Happy."

Ted's eyebrows shot up.

Dave smiled at him, "Yes, just another quiet day's work for us. Come on, we've got some preparations to make."

Ted rolled his eyes and laughed in disbelief.

They made their way to the spot near the fort where Ted had hidden the horses the night before. When they dismounted, Ted looked at him as if to ask, *What kind of preparations can we make here?*

Dave yawned and said, "I sleep, and you keep watch."

Ted kept watch during the afternoon while Dave slept. When Dave woke, Ted lay under the shade of a huge ponderosa pine and slept.

Dave woke him late in the evening, when the dark sky was lit with stars, and spread out what little food they had with them. They ate it hungrily.

Ted wanted to go with him this time, but Dave shook his head. "If I'm not back by daybreak, get the hell out of here, and take Chocolate with you. Come back tomorrow night. If I still don't show up before first light, go on to Livermore and get hold of Jamie Blackfoot. You have the map I drew for you, so you can make it."

Ted nodded, not altogether pleased.

With a quick wave, Dave turned and headed toward the log wall. He was surprised to see no guards on the fence this time.

He headed around to the section that was open the last time and smiled grimly when he saw it still open. Scott had made a mistake once; he wouldn't do it twice. Dave silently moved around the wall to the far side of the fort.

He flicked his rope up to a top post and felt it smoothly hook itself. He'd already tied knots for handholds. With slow, cautious movements, he pulled himself up and over the wall. He crouched low on the small walk that the guards used and scanned the whole area. There were fewer lights than the last time, but he'd expected that. The bunkhouse was dark. He saw the momentary glow of a cigarette by the gap in the fence. As he'd expected, a trap. Good to know he'd figured that one out.

He peered intently at the main house. The back of the big adobe structure was dark. He threw the rope over the other side and climbed down quickly. With a flick of his wrist, the rope jumped off the post and dropped. Dave coiled it and tied it to his belt. The weeds were high, and he crawled safely to the back door. He was not surprised to find it locked. At a nearby window he used his bowie knife and removed the claylike material that surrounded the glass, then gently removed the pane. Stretching his arm inside the window, he groped for the crossbar holding the back door closed. Once he lifted it, he quickly entered the house and replaced the bar.

Inside, he reached out blindly until his hand touched a chair. He sat, pulled out a pair of heavy socks from his pocket, and pulled them on over his boots, grateful for this trick Jamie had taught him.

He tried to remember the arrangement of the house. As he recalled, he was in a storage room. The starlight outside the window offered little help in finding the inside door. He couldn't afford to hurry and knock anything over.

He felt his heart thumping as he reached out slowly with one hand. When it hit nothing, he did the same thing with his foot. He took four such steps and then he heard voices in the next room. Abruptly light gleamed from under a door to his left.

With the light as a beacon, he moved quickly to the door and, pressing his ear against it, tried to listen to the voices, but they had stopped.

He waited for a long moment until finally he felt for the latch, silently lifted it, and peeked out. The door opened into a hallway. There were stairs on his right. Dave knew there were stairs in the front of the house as well, so these must lead to servants' quarters. They were narrow, and he saw they went up to a landing and turned.

Dave hesitated for a moment, listening for any sound. Satisfied with the silence, he slipped out the door and up the stairs. He reached a long hallway with two doors on each side.

When he heard sounds coming from the front stairs, he reached out, opened the first door, and stepped in. He caught the heavy smell of lingering cigar smoke and felt a large wardrobe in a corner. He quickly squeezed between it and the wall just as the door banged open.

Jedd Scott walked in. Dave slid his Adams out and hoped the man wouldn't light the lamp by the bed. Scott pulled off his boots and shoved them aside. He removed keys from his pocket and threw them onto the end table. Then he took off his clothes and tossed them carelessly toward a chair in a corner.

Finally he sat on the bed in his long gray underwear, making a groaning sound. Then he reached out and took a black stogie from the end table, bit off the end, and struck a match. As the match burst into flame, he suddenly saw the intruder. Before Scott could move, Dave silently clipped him on the head with the barrel of his Adams. The man thumped off the bed to the floor.

Dave stomped on the burning match and glared down at Scott with disgust. He wished he could risk shooting him. Instead, he quickly went to the door and checked to be sure the hallway was still empty. Of the three more doors in the hallway, two were open. He went to the closed one and tried the handle. It was locked. He frowned at it, hurried back to Scott's room, and took the keys from the end table. The second key worked.

A woman stood by the window. She jerked back with a gasp. "Mr. Scott doesn't allow anyone in here."

"Are you Henrietta?" he whispered.

She nodded, clearly frightened.

"Listen closely," Dave said quickly. "I'm a friend of Julie's."

"Julie?" She said the name as though it was that of someone long forgotten.

"Yes, I'm a friend. I'm going to get you out of here."

"Friend?" She repeated the word almost mockingly.

"Julie said to tell you to 'make sure you say something in front of the *Amen.*'"

Henrietta paused, and a small smile formed on her face. "Mother was always getting after us—" She stopped and gasped. "Julie really did send you!"

"Yup, she did. We've got to get moving." He glanced down and realized that she had a leg-iron attached to her. He bent down and after some fumbling found the correct key to remove it. Even in the dim light, he could tell how raw her ankle was.

"What are you going to do with me?" she whispered.

"I can't take you home, but I have a friend waiting for us. We're going to get you to Fort Livermore, then bring the troops back to clean the filth out of the valley. You'll need clothes. Pack whatever you can—quickly."

She took a satchel and threw some clothes into it. In a few moments she was ready.

He motioned for her to follow him into Scott's bedroom. She saw the outlaw on the floor.

"Did you kill him?"

"No."

"Then I will," she said firmly.

Dave shook his head. "No, you won't. Believe me, I wouldn't care if you did, but we can't risk it. Too noisy." Even in the darkness, he could see her hate. "Trust me, or stay here with him."

She jerked back. "I'm sorry. It's just been so terrible for so long."

Dave thought she was going to cry, but she didn't. He tied and gagged the still-out-cold Scott. "He looks like a chicken trussed up for cooking."

Henrietta whispered, "Just like a skinny plucked chicken, in his long underwear."

Dave grinned at her, and Henrietta actually smiled.

Dave asked, "Do you know a man named Jamie Blackfoot?"

She shook her head.

"Of course he wouldn't use that name," he muttered to himself. He described him to Henrietta.

"Oh, yes, he left this morning with two others—something about getting some wagons. They won't be back until early next week."

"Good. He'll be safe until I see him."

They went quietly down the back stairs and slipped out into the darkness. The guard by the fence opening was gone, but Dave didn't trust going out that way.

He crept along the wall until he found the ladder the guards used. He took Henrietta's satchel and had her go up the ladder first. At the top of the fence, she peered anxiously over the edge into the black darkness below. Dave followed her up to the ledge, leaned over the wall, and let her satchel drop to the ground. He waited a few moments to be sure no one heard the sound. All was quiet. He pulled the ladder up with some effort and slid it down the other side.

The drop was steeper there, and the ladder went farther down than he expected. "I'll have to help you," he whispered. He picked her up and gingerly lowered her over the wall until her feet touched the top rung. She climbed down quickly. When she was safely down, he glanced around and, satisfied with what he didn't see or hear, crawled over the fence and hurried down the ladder.

She picked up her satchel while he swung the ladder over his shoulder.

"Why are you taking that?" she whispered.

"You never know. I may need it again." He led her to Lonely Creek and hid the ladder under a small underhang. When they reached Ted's position, Dave made a soft hooting sound and heard two quick knocks in return. Ted moved cautiously out of the bushes and approached them, his rifle aimed straight at them.

"It's okay, Ted," Dave said.

The rifle dropped, and he saw Ted's white teeth flash in a smile. "We'd better move fast. Miss Byrne, this is my friend Ted Jones. You ride behind him." Dave placed a hand on Ted's shoulder. "If we run into trouble, we'll use the same ruse as last night."

Ted nodded.

"Were you to blame for that commotion last night?" Henrietta asked in surprise.

"Yeah, why?"

"Well, two men were killed, and five others had to be patched up by the doctor, and they all claimed they were shot by the same man."

"Damnation!" Dave laughed. "That's funny!"

The men mounted, and Ted put out a hand to help Henrietta up. Dave noticed that Ted hadn't taken his eyes off the girl. When she was up on the horse, she put her arms around him, and Dave smiled at Ted's cockeyed grin.

Dave figured if they rode all night and part of the next day, they could be at Fort Livermore and back with the soldiers before anything happened to Julie and her parents. At the same time, he had a bad feeling in his gut, and he didn't like it one bit.

Less than three miles from the turnoff to the hideout, Ted's horse went lame. Dave inspected the animal's leg, bent the hoof up toward its elbow, and gently squeezed the tendon area. The horse immediately flinched. It would never make it over the pass. Dave straightened and rubbed his beard. "That takes care of us getting to Livermore."

Ted shrugged, silently asking what they should do.

Dave nodded thoughtfully. "First, we don't want to be out here at daylight. You take Chocolate and Henrietta back to the hideout. I'll strip your horse down and let her go. I'll get back the Indian way."

Ted looked at Dave, puzzled.

Dave groped in his saddlebag and pulled out a pair of moccasins. Another lesson Jamie Blackfoot had taught him. He would run back to the hideout on foot, only about three miles away.

Ted looked worried as he glanced over his shoulder and waved good-bye.

Dave, however, had forgotten two important points. It was three miles *uphill*, and he hadn't acclimatized to the altitude yet. He was puffing hard and covered with sweat when he staggered up to the cave entrance over an hour and a half later.

Ted stepped out from the trees by the entrance with his rifle at the ready. His smile showed his relief.

Henrietta Byrne was asleep in the cabin. Ted had moved their sleeping gear outside. Dave asked, "What do you think of Henrietta?"

Ted shrugged nonchalantly, but Dave could tell from Ted's grin that she had made an impression on him. Dave knew how he felt. He ran a hand over his growth of beard and wondered if Julie would even know him clean-shaven. "I wish I could take you two with me, but you have enough food to last you until I get back."

Ted nodded.

"I'll bring horses back with me, so your job will be to stay hidden. No fires, and make sure the trap is set by the entrance."

It was almost daylight as he stretched out on his blanket. "I'll leave after dark for Livermore and bring the troops back to clean out this valley as fast as possible." Then he pulled his blanket over him and rolled over, already asleep.

Chapter Eight

Ted shook violently, and then he woke. He'd dreamed the man who had captured him in the mountains was cutting out his tongue. He took a deep breath and exhaled slowly when he realized that it had only been a bad dream. He tried to think of something happy, looked up at the cabin, and smiled.

When the door of the cabin opened, he'd just finished shaving. He splashed some of the cold, soapy water from a pan onto his face and felt the goose bumps bounce down his back.

Henrietta Byrne wore a calico dress with long sleeves and a high neck. She'd pulled her long black hair into a ponytail. She smiled shyly and said, "Good morning."

She glanced at him curiously when he didn't respond. "What's your name?"

Ted took a piece of paper from his shirt pocket and wrote his name on it.

She took the paper from him and, with a puzzled glance, asked, "Can't you talk?"

Ted shook his head.

"Why not?"

He shrugged.

Before she could say anything more, Dave walked into the cabin, looked at the cookstove, and told Henrietta, "We need to get that fire out. The wind's in our favor at the moment, but it can change quickly, and we don't need a smoke signal to mark our location. No more fires until I get back, all right?"

Henrietta glared at Dave and asked angrily, "Why didn't you tell me Ted couldn't speak?"

Dave stopped and stared, at her in surprise. "As I recall, you were asleep when I got in last night." He started putting out the fire. "You didn't notice that last night?"

"I just thought he was shy."

Dave turned to Ted. "Women!"

Ted didn't laugh. Instead, he stood and walked out of the cabin.

Henrietta went to the doorway and watched Ted walk over to the stable.

Dave didn't say anything.

She mumbled softly, "I didn't mean to hurt his feelings."

He turned toward the stove and said, "There's enough heat left in these embers to cook the potatoes."

"You do it," she directed, then turned and walked out to the stable.

Ted was brushing Dave's horse when she walked up behind him. "I'm sorry, Ted. I didn't mean to hurt your feelings."

Ted had his back to her. He shrugged slightly.

"Can you forgive me?" she asked.

He nodded but kept his back to her.

"Good. Come on, let's go have some breakfast." She held out a hand to him.

He turned around and paused, avoiding eye contact with her. He slowly reached out and took her hand.

Dave watched them walk back to the cabin, Henrietta gently holding Ted's hand. Suddenly he sniffed. He jumped to the stove. "Oh, well," he sighed, "I like my potatoes burned."

Dave napped later that day, and well after dark he left for Livermore. Scott's men were patrolling the valley, so it took him longer than he planned to get to the pass. Late the next afternoon, he camped outside Livermore. He didn't want to arrive before dark.

He rode into the town after dusk. With his scruffy beard, tangled hair, and a week's worth of dust and dirt on him, he must surely have a wild appearance about him.

The town of Livermore had grown since the last time he'd been there. New mines had drawn many rough types to the town, and now that the war was over, men were searching for their fortunes.

Dave urged Chocolate toward a small livery run by a Mexican family. He yanked off his saddlebag, pulled his Henry from its sheath, and told the boy in Spanish to rub Chocolate down and feed her well. He flipped the boy a coin and walked to the hotel. There, he laid his gear on the floor by the counter.

The man at the desk looked up at him from behind a pair of thick glasses and asked, "Yeah?"

"Room," Dave said tersely.

The clerk pointed absently toward a pen. Dave picked it up and signed in.

The clerk flipped the book around expertly and demanded, "Fifty cents a night, in advance." He glanced down at the name. "Uh . . . Mr. Jackson."

Dave placed a dollar on the desk, and the clerk gave him a key and change. When he picked up his gear, Dave glanced at a man sitting in an overstuffed chair, smoking a cigar. He almost smiled when Jamie Blackfoot started to cough into a cloud of smoke. Dave started up the stairs, saying nothing.

He opened the door of his room cautiously, looked around, and walked in. The room was small, stuffy, and dusty. The window faced the back of the hotel. He dropped his saddlebag on top of the bed, tucked the Henry under the mattress, and walked back down to the lobby. Jamie was gone, but that didn't surprise him.

Dave asked the clerk, "Anywhere I can get a bath and shave around here this time of night?"

The clerk didn't look up from the paper he was reading but replied sarcastically, "How the hell should I know?"

Dave leaned his hands on top of the counter and stared down at the clerk.

When the clerk realized that Dave was glaring at him, he gulped and pretended to concentrate on the paper. The longer Dave stared, the more nervous the clerk became. The clerk finally swallowed, pointed across the street, and said weakly, "Schulz' Barbershop. They stay open late for the miners."

"Good." Dave had an amused smile on his face as he walked out of the hotel.

Before Dave went to the barbershop, he walked to a small

general store and bought a complete set of new clothes. He carried them with him to the barbershop. The street was starting to fill with people, since the supper hour was over, yet no customers were in the barbershop.

The shave felt fine, but not as relaxing as the bath. Dave settled up to his neck in warm, soapy water. It was the first bath he'd had in weeks, and he planned to enjoy it to its fullest. He heard shots close by but was half-asleep in the warm water and paid no attention.

While he was in the bath, he had his boots cleaned and polished. After dressing, he gazed at his image in the mirror and smiled. It felt odd to be clean and in new clothes.

It was time to meet Jamie at the Golden Spur. Dave walked into the crowded saloon and scanned the heavy smoke for anyone who might recognize him. The long bar ran the length of the building on the left. At the back of the building was a small, crudely built stage, near stairs going up to the second floor. Dave could barely hear the sound of the piano player on the stage over the crowd's noise. Gambling and drinking tables filled the rest of the space.

He moved to the end of the bar and ordered a whiskey. He sipped it slowly and thought about another time he'd met Jamie in a bar. Four men had died by Dave's Adams that night. Dave shook his head to erase the memory. A young dance-hall woman walked up to him and asked, "Buy me a drink?"

He started to shake his head no but suddenly changed his mind when he glanced at her. "Sure."

She motioned to the bartender, who poured her a drink.

Dave looked at her closely. She reminded him of someone. Her jet black hair and sharp features made it seem likely that she had Indian blood in her. Her face had a tired look, but she still held a beauty about her. Dave also felt danger. Perhaps, he thought, it was her black eyes that seemed to see right into his soul.

"Want to sit at a table?" she asked.

Dave nodded. He grabbed his drink and followed her to a table.

"My name's Sally. What's yours?"

"Dave Jackson. Everybody calls me Davey, though." That came

out so easily, Dave almost smiled at the often-used fake name. He held a chair out for Sally. For a moment he thought she wasn't going to sit down.

"The last time a man helped me sit down, it was a Yankee major with a wife and two kids."

Dave smiled and said, "Were you drinking tea then too?"

She glanced down at her drink. "You don't miss much, do you?"

Dave finished his drink and waved for the bartender to bring him another. "No, ma'am," Dave said slowly. "We've all surely had to grow up too fast."

The bartender brought them fresh drinks.

She asked Dave, "Switch drinks with me for second, will you? This tea is turning me green. The boss doesn't want any of us drinking on the job."

Dave did, and she took two sips. "I don't drink much, but that tea is really bad."

Dave nodded at her when he tasted the tea. It was bad.

She reached over and took his hand. "Would you like to go upstairs with me?"

Dave shook his head. "I'm happy sitting here with you." He took his whiskey back from her.

She looked around cautiously and said in a whisper, "Jamie's upstairs."

Dave's eyebrows shot up. He still sensed something sinister in her gaze. She stared at him with unblinking black eyes.

"Let's go," he said.

He stood and helped her up from her chair. Then he grasped her arm firmly. To anyone who might look, he was being gentlemanly, but Sally would know she was being guided by him as they walked up the stairs.

They walked down a dark corridor that made Dave edgy. She took out a key and opened a door at the end of the hallway. When she had it half open, he grabbed her, pulled his Adams, and slid through the door, using her as a shield. He kicked the door shut.

"That you, Davey?" Jamie's voice called out from a doorway to the right. His voice sounded strange.

"Yeah, Jamie. You all right?"

"Aye. Come on in."

Dave's features hardened. He pushed Sally against the door and quickly locked it with her key. He pulled his bowie knife with his left hand and put his arm around her so the blade rested lightly against her throat.

"Sally, my love," Dave whispered, "you make one foolish move, and your head will leave your body." Her face told him that she understood.

They walked into the room, Sally in front. Jamie lay in the bed. Two men stood on the far side of it. Neither held a gun.

Jamie watched him come in and laughed painfully. "Gently, laddie. I told the major you were a cautious man."

Dave glanced around the room. A small screen stood in one corner, and he said threateningly, "Well, Major, as Jamie says, I'm a cautious man. If you move that screen, and no one's there, then you just might live out the evening."

The major twisted his head and said, "Put your gun away, Captain, and come on out."

Jamie smiled again and said, "Aye, Davey. You make me proud. That's all of them. Now, put that damn bowie down before you slice my daughter."

Dave slid the knife back into its scabbard but kept the Adams leveled at the man who came out from behind the screen. "What do you mean, 'daughter'?" Dave asked. "And what the hell are you doing in bed? That cigar make you sick?"

"Scott must've got wind of who I was. Right after I saw you, his men plugged me. I played dead, and they took off. Then I crawled over here." Jamie grinned.

Dave still armed his Adams at the captain.

"I'd better introduce you before you shoot everybody here." Jamie motioned with his eyes. "That's Major Bates from Fort Livermore."

Dave nodded briefly, still suspicious.

"The one beside him is a special agent with Wells Fargo, Jim Bates."

Dave nodded again and asked, "Related?"

"Brothers," Jim Bates said.

Jamie pointed to the man by the screen. "That's Captain Humberto Filmore Junior, but he prefers everyone call him Slim."

Dave finally put his Adams away and held out his hand to Slim. They shook. "Seems I should know you."

Slim agreed. "I was on a wagonload of prisoners-of-war in Tupelo. You attacked it and set us free."

"Yes, of course." Dave grinned.

"I never was able to thank you."

"Consider it done." Dave turned his attention back to Jamie. "How bad are you shot?" He lifted the blanket and saw the bloody bandages wrapped around his friend's chest and stomach. "You're not going to be much help, but I've seen you worse."

"Aye, but I'm getting tired of all these bulletholes. You get to have the fun this time."

"That's what you told me the last time. And as I recall, there was no 'fun,' yet you seemed to think that was very funny."

"Still do," Jamie said in a whisper.

"Major Kramer," the major said, "we have some serious problems. We realize you aren't under obligation to the Army anymore, but we need your help. With what Blackfoot has told me about you and your battle experience, you are an answer to a prayer. I'm afraid my experience in dealing with this sort of situation is very limited."

"Aye, I've already told the major you would help," Jamie said weakly.

"That doesn't surprise me. You were always volunteering me." He grinned down at Jamie. "Thought you'd just sleep this one out and let me do all the work again, huh?" To the major he said, "If Jamie says I'll help, then you've got my help. How about filling me in?"

The major nodded. "The man, Jedd Scott, was a Union guerrilla fighter. He turned renegade about six months before the war ended. He stole a big stagecoach shipment of gold coins and came here. He found Quiet Valley, we think, just by accident—by our reckoning, right after the epidemic, so there was hardly anyone left in the valley."

Dave interrupted. "Jamie filled me in on that. But what about the Byrne family? And why didn't he just kill off the rest of the people in Quiet Valley? I can see why he kept the doctor alive, but why the others?"

Major Bates nodded. "Good questions. I personally think Scott is mad. He seriously seems to be planning to become a king of his own country. He'd need workers, so I think that's why he decided to keep the people left in the valley alive—as his servants or slaves. At least, that's my theory.

"As for the Byrne family, he has them take care of the cattle and raise food for his men. I imagine he has something on Byrne to hold them there. Of course, he's also holding one of the daughters captive, so that might be it."

"Was," Dave said.

"Was?" Jamie asked softly.

"I got her out."

"You didn't get yourself locked into the icehouse again, did you?"

"Nah, I just went right into the main house and tapped Scott on the head with my Adams."

"You killed him?"

"Nope. Would've made too much noise and alerted his men. Hog-tied him and left him in his long underwear on the floor of his bedroom."

"He's a mighty proud man. I sure would have enjoyed seeing the look on his face when somebody found him. That's going to upset him something fierce."

"Yup, I imagine so. I also saw an old friend of yours. Remember Happy?"

"Old scar-mouth." Jamie laughed painfully. "Aye, maybe he was the one who marked me to be shot down."

"I suspect he'd just recently arrived."

"Someone had to mark me," Jamie said, his eyes closed again. "Not sure who else it could have been."

"Well, you have made a few enemies in your time."

"Aye. Too many."

Dave asked Major Bates, "How about the rest of the story? Why the delay? Why don't you just go in and shoot Scott down?"

The major shook his head. "It's one hell of a tricky situation. We're not sure where he has the gold. Second, a gang of Bishop's boys are riding in to join him. Worst of all, we are seriously low on troops and ammunition here at the fort."

"Maybe you could pick them off in small bunches," Dave said.

The major nodded in agreement. "We know that Scott's low on guns and ammunition, thanks to you, but as I said, so are we. When we get our new shipment, we plan to attack. I've asked for more men from Fort Smith, but they're low on troops also."

"Where are your new rifles and ammo?" Dave asked.

"On their way here."

Dave ran a hand over his face and said, "I'll bet you a hundred dollars cash they never make it to your fort."

The major frowned at his brother, then down at Jamie.

Jamie had his eyes closed but was very much awake. "Aye, that's what I told him too. But he blabbed on about their being secure, nobody knowing about them and how well they'll be guarded."

Dave asked Jamie, "Did Scott ever mention the wagons coming in?"

"He kept things very close to his vest. I wasn't even sure why he sent the three of us here. Just told me to come here and wait for instructions." Jamie opened one eye. "He never really trusted me, right from the first. Maybe he didn't like my earthy smell."

Dave grinned and shook his head slowly. "Major, you say you're low on ammo. How low?"

"Next to nothing. We never had much trouble out here, so they rationed us real low near the end of the war."

"And you think you've kept the wagons' arrival a secret, huh?"

"Absolutely."

Dave shook his head at the major. "Two nights ago, I overhead Scott talking about taking some wagons. I didn't know what he was talking about then, but now it makes sense. Then tonight the barber told me you have two wagonloads with six guards and two drivers coming in tomorrow. Is that your secret?"

"How could anyone . . ." Major Bates gasped, unable to complete his thought.

"All right," Dave sighed, "we'll worry about the rifles and ammo first. You get back to the fort and get a detachment together to go out and meet and escort those wagons. We've got to get to them before Scott does. I'll get my stuff from the hotel and meet you at the fort."

Major Bates, Jim Bates, and Slim left by crawling out the bedroom window onto a back staircase.

Dave smiled down fondly at Jamie. "You take care. I'll be back."

Jamie opened one eye, and a slight grin crossed his face. "You sure smell pretty."

Dave laughed and turned to go.

"Ride on the clouds, laddie," Jamie whispered.

Dave stopped and turned back. He tried not to show his concern. "Ride on the clouds, old friend." Dave made two fists and crossed his arms against his chest. It was the first sign Jamie had ever taught him, and it meant affection for the other person. Since Jamie wasn't a demonstrative man, Dave always felt it was Jamie's way of saying how much he cared without actually having to say it.

Jamie nodded and closed his eyes.

Sally followed Dave out into the front room. He unlocked the door and handed back her key.

"I'd better mess your hair some," Sally told him. "You don't want to look too tidy when you go back down. The men will think you didn't have a good time with me." She ran her hands through his hair and then pulled his face down to hers and kissed him quickly. "I can do better when you're not in such a hurry."

Dave looked at her for a long moment, nodded slightly, and hurried down the hall, glad to be away from her. He found it hard to believe she was Jamie's daughter.

Back at the hotel, he slipped out of his room the back way and hurried, unseen, to the stable with his saddlebag and Henry. Riding in the shadows behind the buildings, he took his time leaving town to be sure he wasn't followed. He was glad for the rest he'd gotten before riding into town. He ran a hand across one cheek. At least he had a shave, a bath, and new clothes, so if, as he suspected, it was going to be another long night, it was good not to feel all itchy and grubby.

Chapter Nine

It took almost an hour to get from the town of Livermore to Fort Livermore, and although it was dark, the road was easy to follow.

Dave rode relaxed in the saddle, deep in thought. Major Bates was unwise to try to count on taking Scott's whole bunch at once. If the men were all guerrilla fighters, they would rip, run, and hide, then do it again and again until Bates had no troops left. And for the major to expect Scott not to know about the guns and ammo coming in—that was plain foolishness.

Dave rubbed the back of his neck and shook his head sadly. This could turn into one hell of a mess. If Fort Livermore could not bring the fight to Scott in the next couple of days, he would have to ride back to Quiet Valley with enough horses for Ted and the Byrne family. He had to get them safely all out of the valley. Once he had them out, he could go back and deal with Scott himself.

Dave was surprised when he got to Fort Livermore to find the gate open and no guards on duty. He saw Jim Bates standing outside the major's office waiting for him. From the sour look on Jim's face, Dave knew there was trouble.

Dave said bluntly, "Let's have it."

Jim shook his head. "We were almost back here when a rider rode up and told us the ammo wagons were under attack. Before I could stop him, he rode in, rallied the whole company, and raced out of here."

"Damnation!" Dave exclaimed. "Who was the rider?"

Jim shrugged. "I don't know. Maybe not even Army. You think it's a trap too, don't you?"

"I reckon it doesn't matter what I think. He took everyone?" Jim nodded.

"He didn't leave any guards at all?" Dave asked in amazement.

"Me."

"Damnation! No guards. Unbelievable."

"Maybe Scott won't know the fort is empty?" Jim suggested hopefully.

"Not a chance. Scott will have left a spotter to see if his ruse worked. The first man will take the major and the troops on a long, roundabout way to give the spotter time to get back and tell Scott, so he can set up the ambush."

"Do you think he already has the ammo wagons?"

"Not sure." Dave tried to think what Scott might do. "If Scott can wipe out the troops, then picking off the wagons will be easy." He shook his head. "If the major had been able to join up with the ammo wagons . . ." He stopped, frowned, and asked Jim, "There's no way anyone could have heard us talking back in Jamie's room, is there?"

"The walls are paper thin, but we didn't see anyone around. Why?"

"It's as though Scott knew our plans. It'll be a lot easier to ambush the troops and then go after the wagons. Together the wagons and troops make a formidable force, particularly if they were expecting to be attacked."

"I don't see how he could have found out," Jim said. "We all left right after we talked and came directly here. He'd have to have been close by to find out so quickly."

Dave nodded uncertainly. "Curious. Well, we have to figure that Scott knows this fort is unguarded. I'm thinking he'll send some of his men here to ransack it, knowing it's all but deserted, perhaps even burn it down."

"Anything we can do to stop it?"

Dave glanced around. "Maybe we can bait them into a little trap of our own. Scott won't spare many men for the fort. He wants that ammo too much. Who's left?"

"Wives and children."

"We'll need to move everybody into one building."

"Already have," Jim replied, as he motioned to the main building behind him.

"Good. Glad someone is thinking around here."

"Don't be too hard on my brother. He means well."

Dave nodded and said bitterly, "I've seen too many good men die because of officers who meant well."

Jim winced at Dave's words but didn't say more.

It took Dave a few moments to explain the trap to Jim and build two quick barricades. After that, all they could do was wait and see if his hunch was correct.

Dave waited behind the front gate. There was no moon. The cold night air seemed to eat slowly through his clothes. He wished that he had a blanket to throw over his shoulders. A couple of crickets made their chirps in a quiet, systematic way. Dave crossed his arms over his chest and tucked his hands under his armpits to keep them warm.

Suddenly, the crickets stopped, and Dave felt a cold sensation run down his spine. A horse shook its head outside the partly opened gate. Dave felt the gate being quietly shoved all the way open. Once opened, it blocked his view. He remained calm but ready. He heard horses slowly entering the fort.

This would be the hard part. Jim's first shot would be the signal. Dave would slam the gate and, hopefully, trap the riders inside. If there were more than four or five, it might not turn out well. Dave raised a foot and braced it against the gate.

Three shots rang out.

Dave shoved the gate closed with his foot. He rammed the latch into the slot and leaped behind a barricade he'd built on the other side.

Two of Scott's men rode back to the gate and cursed. Dave rose to a half-crouched position and fired his Adams three times. The horses galloped wildly back into the fort, their saddles empty. One man staggered to his feet and tried to aim his gun at Dave. Dave fired another shot that spun the gunman into a lopsided somersault.

Dave waited a moment, then moved out and checked the two men to make sure they were dead. He saw Jim bent over another body in the parade ground.

A horse was on its side, moaning feebly. Dave took his Adams and shot it once in the head to put it out of its misery.

Jim walked up with Dave's Henry and said, "That's a damn good rifle you've got there."

Dave looked around him and said, "Tell the women it's safe. I'll move the bodies behind that small building over to the left."

"Right."

It took half an hour to move the three dead men and the dead horse out of the way. And once again came the waiting.

The sky was slowly turning a red-orange color, erasing the night darkness, when the first trooper came in. He rode in exhausted, his head almost touching the mane of his horse, his clothes red with blood.

Dave told Jim to keep watch. He hurried to the wounded trooper and carried him into a nearby bunkhouse. In the next two hours they came in by twos and threes until sixteen of them were back. The fort didn't have a doctor assigned to it, so Dave sent one uninjured trooper into Livermore to bring back the town doctor.

When Dave was finally able to get away from the makeshift hospital, he sent a private out to relieve Jim. He told the private to have Jim meet him in the major's office.

Dave sank wearily into the major's chair and, after checking the drawers, found a whiskey bottle and glasses. He poured two glasses and drank one in two quick gulps. Jim walked in and took the drink Dave handed him without a word.

Jim slumped into a chair, rubbed his eyes with his fingers, and asked, "Is my brother dead?"

Dave nodded. "Yes. I heard he was the first man to get it. Never knew what hit him. They rode right into a trap."

"Captain Filmore?"

"Couple of the troopers said he was alive when they left. He told them to get out while he covered their retreat. Hell of a man."

Tears formed in Jim's eyes.

A woman—Mrs. Bates, Dave soon realized—opened the door

and walked in. When she saw Jim weeping, she burst into tears and ran into his arms. They tried to comfort each other.

Dave walked out quietly. A sergeant hurried over to him and asked, "Excuse me, sir, but Captain Filmore told me another major was joining us as soon as we got back with the wagons. You aren't in uniform, but Mrs. Bates said you were an officer. The men would like to know if you are in command."

Dave nodded tiredly. "Yeah, that's right. I'm Major Kramer. I'll take over until we can work out something better."

"Thank you, sir." He saluted.

Dave saluted him back. "Sergeant, how many men have we who aren't wounded?"

"Three, sir. Myself, the private on guard duty, and Corporal Metzler. Metzler was the man you sent to Livermore for the doctor."

"How many wounded?"

"Thirteen. Three real bad."

Dave shook his head, "Okay, Sergeant, thanks. You go get some rest."

"Thank you, sir." The sergeant saluted again, turned to go, stopped, and turned back. "You know, we never had a chance."

"I know. It's all right. Get some rest."

Dave climbed the ladder to the lookout beside the gate. The private nodded at him and shook his head when Dave asked him if he had seen anything.

Then he grabbed Dave's arm and pointed up the road. A stream of dust slowly rose along the ground, looking white and filmy in the early-morning light.

Dave turned to the private and said, "Get the sergeant and Jim Bates."

"Yes, sir."

Dave watched the dust cloud slowly billow toward the fort. Underneath the dust cloud, he saw a wagon being driven hard and fast. The driver wore a blue uniform. Another trap? Dave checked his Henry.

From the right of the road, a group of Scott's riders galloped out of the brush, trying to cut off the wagon. Dave quickly decided that whoever was driving the wagon must not be a friend of Scott. He brought his Henry up to his shoulder and as fast as he could fired off multiple shots. The distance was too great for him to hit any of the riders, but the speed and closeness of the shots caused them to scatter and turn back.

Dave saw that Slim Filmore was the wagon driver. Dave yelled down for Jim and the sergeant to open the gate. The horses charged into the fort, dripping with sweat and with nostrils flared to catch the wind.

Slim rolled off the wagon seat and wiped the sweat from his dust-covered forehead. His hat was missing. A wounded trooper fell out of the wagon into Slim's arms. Slim laid the man down by the front wheel and hurried around to the back of the wagon to help another wounded trooper.

The private clambered up the ladder into the lookout tower, expecting a tough fight from the men chasing his captain. But when he looked out, all he saw was a dust cloud moving away from the fort. Clearly Scott's men didn't intend to attack the fort. The private exclaimed excitedly, "You must have put the fear of God into them, the way you were shooting."

Dave tossed his rifle up to the private. "Perhaps, but you keep a close watch in case they circle back. I've reloaded it."

Slim's wife rushed out of the makeshift hospital and held Slim so close, Dave wasn't sure Slim could even breathe. She finally released him, kissed him hard, and then gently touched his cheek with her fingers. "I knew you'd come home to me." She kissed him again, softly this time, and said, "I've got to doctor your men."

He nodded at her and then glanced at Dave.

"Was getting a mite worried about you," Dave said.

Slim took a deep breath and let it out slowly. "I had my own doubts. How bad are we?"

"Bad. With the two wounded you brought back, you've got fifteen injured and four, counting you, who made it back without being shot. The rest are still out there."

Slim's head dropped to his chest, "Eleven good men and the major. Does Mrs. Bates know yet?"

"Yeah. Must have taken some doing, getting that ammo wagon."

Slim almost smiled. "They were so damn busy killing us off,

they only left one guard. I tried to destroy the other wagon but couldn't do that and get this one too."

Dave put a hand on Slim's shoulder. "You did a hell of a job out there. Don't feel bad for what you couldn't do."

Slim nodded.

"Go and get some rest. We'll talk later."

Late in the afternoon, Slim walked into the major's office. Jim Bates was asleep in a rocking chair in the corner but woke when he came in. Dave sat in the major's chair, his feet propped up on the desk. Slim couldn't tell if Dave had been asleep, but he saw that Dave's eyes followed him the moment he stepped into the room, although his head didn't move. Right at that moment, Slim realized how careful Dave really was. He never seemed to let his guard down, wherever he was. Slim took a seat in front of the desk.

"I just checked the wounded. Two men have died, but the doctor said he thinks the rest will pull through. I wonder if we got even one of Scott's men," Slim said sadly. "And what of my men still out there? Do we just leave them?"

Dave pulled his feet from the desk, sat up, and nodded thoughtfully. "We'll need to collect the bodies. Scott's men likely won't leave any wounded." He was silent for a few moments. "But get one man to ride out and see if anyone is alive. If not, have him go on into Livermore and get the gravedigger to go back and pick up the bodies."

"The major too?" Slim asked.

" 'Fraid so."

Slim looked sick.

"I understand your feelings. I wish it didn't have to be so, but we have things to do that can't wait. Right now we've got to protect the living. You can be sure Scott's not going to waste time."

Jim Bates nodded. "It doesn't matter, Slim. My brother would want us to stop Scott. At the moment, that means getting the Army fully involved."

Dave agreed. "Jim's right. Scott's move against the fort and killing a third of a company, not even counting Jim's brother, makes it imperative for the Army to move."

"I can get Wells Fargo to put pressure on the commander at Fort Smith to bring at least four companies of cavalry in."

Dave said, "If they have that many. Besides, I don't think it will take much pressure. The Army gets mighty upset when they start losing their officers, particularly in an ambush. Unfortunately, it will take at least a week to get word to Fort Smith and another seven or eight days to get back with anyone." Dave stood and looked at the map on the wall. "You know Scott will have men waiting for you. He knows you're going to have to go to Fort Smith for help."

Slim moved over to the map. "Where? Where do you think he'll hit us?"

Dave ran a finger slowly along the route to Fort Smith. "Here . . . or here . . . maybe here." Dave looked at Slim. "You reckon you can make it?"

"I can make it."

Dave agreed with a brief smile. "Yes, I reckon you can. Jim, you going with him?"

"Absolutely. I've got a few scores of my own to settle."

"Remember, you're dealing with guerrilla fighters." He pointed back to the map. "They'll try to trap you in boxes or hit you at night, when you're asleep."

Slim nodded. "How many will they use?"

"Hard to tell, since they didn't get a chance to burn the fort down and only got half the ammunition they wanted." Dave paused, thinking. "Perhaps six or eight. Maybe a few more, but I doubt it. He's starting to lose men too. He lost three here, and he didn't expect that. I'm hoping stealing Henrietta Byrne right out of his house has spooked him a little too. I don't think he feels as safe as he used to. That could help hold down the number of men he'll send out, but we don't really know how many men he has."

"We'll leave tonight."

"Take that feisty sergeant with you and the private who was up on the lookout with me. That will be four of you. Each of you take an extra horse. If they jump you, take the fresher horse and leave the other. Go light on gear and heavy on ammo. If you do get into a gunfight, you don't want to run out of bullets."

"What about you?" Slim asked.

"I've got to get back to Quiet Valley."

"How do we protect the fort while we're all gone?" Slim asked.

"Good point." Dave nodded. "All right, give that Corporal Metzler a chance at command. He seems like a good man. They'd love to get that wagon you brought in, but they won't likely try a direct assault. Since their first attack against the fort didn't work, maybe they aren't as sure about how many troops we have left here. We close up the fort and don't let anyone in until one of us gets back. There's plenty of food and water."

He thought for a moment. "At night, though, they might make a try for it. Build fires all around the fort, about two hundred yards out. Like the wagon trains. Keep them burning all night. Tough for anyone to sneak up that way. The men who are hurt the least can stay up all night, keeping watch. Stick the rifles you brought in through the posts, as if someone is there."

Dave glanced at his hat. "Place hats on the posts by the rifles too. That might fake out Scott's men and make them think we have more troops than we do. Having the rifles up there and loaded will give our people more firepower, if there is an attack. The women and the wounded men who can should keep watch by day."

"Why don't you wait for us?"

"I've got to get the Byrne family out and any of the other hostages Scott is holding. That damned fool may just decide to kill everybody and take off."

"Let me find some volunteers to go back with you, Dave," Slim suggested.

"You don't have any," Dave reminded him. "But I do need horses. At least four to bring the Byrnes out, and one for Ted."

"You've got them."

"Good, I'll pick five, but I'll leave the best ones for you. Oh, yes, Slim, I told Jim the back way into Quiet Valley. That should save you a half day. I'll try to be back with the Byrne family in a week or less. Then Ted and I will go after the other hostages. If we can get them, fine. If we can't, we'll meet you at the top of the pass fourteen or fifteen days from now."

"We won't let you down," Slim promised.

The three men shook hands warmly. Dave took his hat from the chair and nodded. "See you gents around. Watch your backs once you're out on the road."

Dave picked out five horses and rode quickly to Livermore. He wanted to check in on Jamie again; he needed to find out how many men Scott had left. He was angry with himself for not asking Jamie earlier.

The Golden Spur looked empty from the outside, but when he walked in, Dave noticed that everyone was either on the stairway or upstairs in the hall. Dave pushed his way through the mob until he came to Sally's door. He pushed his way into the back room.

Jamie was hanging over the side of the bed. Someone had used a shotgun on him, at close range. A man bending over the body glanced up and asked, "Anybody know him?"

Dave didn't answer but turned and raced out of the saloon. Once on the street, he paused and took a couple of slow, deep breaths. His insides were churning. He wanted to kick something or scream, but he did neither.

Wiping the tears from his eyes with the back of one hand, he hurried to the back of the saloon, where he'd left the horses. He was going to miss Jamie. He was going to miss him a lot. Mounting, he glanced up at the clouds floating through the night sky and said softly, "Ride with the clouds, old friend." Tears started rolling down his cheeks as he rode out of town.

What of Sally? Where was she? He thought about going back to find her. But what he needed to do was try to save the Byrne family. Sally would have to wait. She was tough. Maybe she was hiding out.

Things were starting to blow up in his face. Good men were dying. This was too much like the war he'd thought he'd left behind. He didn't like it at all.

Chapter Ten

Anger—the deep, bitter anger of a man who has just seen the bloody body of a murdered friend—drove him hard. He rode long into the night, and only when he realized the horses were starting to falter did he stop.

The horses were covered with sweaty foam, and he cursed himself for being so hard on them. He stopped by a small stream and rubbed each one down. When they were cool, he fed and watered them. Only until all six animals were cared for did he give his own needs any thought.

He wanted a cup of hot coffee to help kill the high-desert chill, but he knew a fire would be a beacon to too many. He took a swig of water from his canteen and chewed on four small pieces of dried beef. The desert was silent tonight, as silent as the blackness surrounding him.

He had trouble sleeping and rose early. This time he fixed a tiny fire and quickly made coffee. He paced back and forth as he drank it. He had a strong sense of danger concerning Ted and Henrietta.

Again he pushed the horses, but the extra animals slowed him down coming over the narrow pass, and it was late in the afternoon before he reached the creek bed leading to the hideout.

As he slowly moved the horses up the creek bed, his sense of foreboding about Ted and Henrietta returned.

When he neared the hideout, he saw two horses standing quietly outside the opening to the cave. The bushes hiding the entrance had been torn away.

In one motion, Dave dismounted from Chocolate and pulled

the Henry from its sheath. He moved the horses down the creek bed, hid them, and crept back to the entrance. He made a perfect target for anyone waiting for him, but he didn't care.

Dave shoved the lever down on the Henry and felt the .44 cartridge ram home as he pulled the lever back. He started into the cavern but stopped a few feet inside.

Someone was coming out through the cave.

He spun and hurried out. Hiding behind a large bush, he waited.

One minute passed . . . then two . . . three . . . four. Dave blinked to relax his tension. He half rose to start back into the cave when he heard a woman yell and somebody cuss. He ducked back down.

Two of Scott's gunmen backed out of the cave, dragging Henrietta. She was kicking and scratching like a wildcat. She broke loose and ran up the creek bank. That was all Dave needed.

He opened fire. The explosion of the Henry echoed loudly. One gunman was hit in the chest and fell backward. He tried to crawl away on his hands and knees but was hit three more times and was dead before his face smashed into the ground. Four screaming bullets flattened the other gunman to the dirt.

Henrietta raced to Dave and fell sobbing into his arms, gasping that the men had killed Ted.

Dave put his arm around Henrietta, and they hurried back into the cavern. They ran through the darkness, and as they reached the other end, Dave suddenly shoved Henrietta to the ground and dove to the opposite side of the tunnel. In almost the same instant, a shot exploded over them, back down into the passageway.

Dave twisted and saw Ted, badly bloodied, standing five feet from the cave entrance with his Henry raised.

Henrietta spoke softly. "Ted, it's all right. Mr. Kramer's here."

Ted's face twisted as though he was trying to understand what she said. He took one step forward and fell heavily to the ground.

Dave carried him to the spring. He washed the blood out of his eyes and quickly cleaned the deep furrow a bullet had sliced across his forehead. Then he wrapped Ted's head with a piece of cloth Henrietta gave him. Dave picked Ted up in his arms, carried him into the cabin, and laid him on the bottom bunk.

Ted had been shot in the leg, chest, and neck in addition to the graze across his forehead. Dave patched the leg wound. That bullet had passed through without breaking any bones. It was the chest and neck wounds that worried him. Both bullets were still in Ted, and unless he could get him to a doctor, he wouldn't have a chance.

Dave said to Henrietta, "You're going to have to take care of him while I get help."

"Mr. Kramer, it won't do any good. They already sent another man back."

"Damnation!" He looked at her and said, "I'd better get the guns from those two. We're going to need them."

Dave hurried back out of the passageway to the dead gunmen. He pulled off their gun belts and slung them over his shoulder. He pulled two Sharps rifles from the horses and found a box of shells in one of the saddlebags.

Ted was half awake when Dave came back into the cabin. He tried to smile up at Dave, but even that effort was too much for him. His eyes closed again.

Henrietta had rebandaged Ted's head while Dave collected the guns. She washed the blood off her hands while Dave poured a cup of lukewarm coffee and drank it in large gulps.

Henrietta asked, "Does he have a chance?"

Dave shook his head and said, "I don't think so. He's shot up bad. He needs a doctor. If we try to get him to Livermore, the trip over the mountains will finish him. If we stay, Scott will. Damnation! A poor selection of choices." He threw the coffee cup across the room.

Henrietta said softly, "We can't stay here."

"Yeah, I know. We can't stay, we can't go." He sighed and tapped his right fist into his open left palm, while he tried to think. "Okay, Miss Byrne, get what gear we need, and I'll see if I can hold Ted together long enough for us to find a new hiding place."

"Do you know where we can go?"

"No, but I'll find something."

Henrietta hesitated before speaking. "Mr. Kramer?"

"Yes?"

"I know Ted trusted you. Well, I do too."

Dave reached over and gently squeezed her shoulder. "Thanks. Let's just pray Ted is tough enough to hold on."

Dave cradled Ted in his arms as he rode. Henrietta rode one of the gunmen's horses. They moved slowly, yet Ted moaned softly with each step of the horse, and Dave felt his blood running over his hand. The chest wound was bleeding again.

He halted and scanned the area. The harsh, rocky path appeared as inhospitable as an angry grizzly. The trail went higher and higher into the mountains. Finally, if a person knew where to look, came a dangerous, narrow pass that led out of the valley. It was jagged, high-mountain country yet not rocky enough to hide in for any length of time.

He studied the trail again. He reckoned two miles or more to the pass. If they could make it there, they'd have a chance, yet even if they did, he knew Ted wouldn't make it all the way to Livermore.

Henrietta exclaimed, "Look!" She pointed down the trail they had just traveled.

Two men were slowly following them. Dave peered at them. "They've seen us. Their horses are pretty well beat, but they'll still catch us before we reach the pass. I'll draw you a map. You can make it through the pass alone. From there, it's a fast ride to Livermore."

"What about you and Ted?"

He squinted intently up the trail, trying to remember anyplace they could hide. Suddenly he recalled a high shelf not far from them where he'd found shelter from a thunderstorm that had swept over the mountains when he was hunting long ago. A small but deep shelf, about twenty feet up the side of a cliff, with a large overhang—not the best place for a fight, but better than being out in the open. It looked like a cave but it wasn't, just a deep gash in the side of the mountain. At least they would have their backs protected.

"We'll hole up in a shelf area I remember near here."

"I'll stay with you," she said determinedly.

"Don't be foolish, Miss Byrne. It will be two weeks before the troopers can get here. There's no sense in all of us getting killed. If you get to Livermore, you might be able to bring back help."

She shook her head. "It will take too long."

Dave knew she was right.

"Ted needs me. You need me. I can shoot a rifle. I can help. I can't run away."

Dave shook his head. She was right, but he would hate to see her get killed too.

It took them another twenty minutes to get to the shelf. Dave carried Ted up and laid him gently on an old blanket at the back of the underhang. He looked at their supplies and decided they had enough food and water for two or three days—and enough ammunition for maybe half a day.

The two men following them had disappeared, but Dave knew that at least one had remained behind to keep watch. The other man was likely riding back to the Bowman Fort to tell Scott that Ted Jones wasn't the only one involved in all his troubles these last few days.

They had no choice but to wait. Ted moaned softly. Henrietta tended him gently, never leaving his side.

Dave found enough rocks to build a fortification in front of them, but he knew it wasn't going to be pleasant tomorrow. Scott would pour bullets into the shelf, and that meant bullets ricocheting around them, if not into them. Still, in the morning Scott would have the sun glaring in his eyes.

Who knew?

Chapter Eleven

The sun set quickly, and just as quickly they had only the stars for light. One horse tied below the shelf whinnied, and Dave knew they had a visitor.

It was far too soon for the rest of Scott's men to have made it back, so Dave decided it must be the lone guard trying to be resourceful and run off the horses. Dave took out his Adams and crawled silently down the path leading from the shelf.

The guard crept silently toward the horses. When he reached them, he glanced up at the ledge above him. Satisfied that he hadn't been seen, he stood and reached for the reins.

Just as his hand touched Chocolate's reins, Dave fired. The man was dead before his body hit the ground. The horses leaped wildly and pulled at their reins.

Dave continued down the path and quieted the horses. He stripped the gun belt from the outlaw, pulled the body away from the horses, then hurried back to the shelf.

Two hours later, he heard noises again—this time the sound of many horsemen. Henrietta was asleep beside Ted. He let her sleep. Scott couldn't be sure of the shelf's location or of how badly wounded Ted was. Dave felt certain the Undertaker would wait until daylight to make his move.

Just before daylight, Dave woke Henrietta. He had a plan he'd been thinking about through the night, and he needed her help. He explained it to her quickly, and even in the darkness, he saw her reaction to its desperation.

Dave checked Ted's Henry and handed it to Henrietta. He slipped his big socks over his boots, took his own rifle, grabbed two of the extra revolvers, and silently moved down the path. The path leading to the front of the shelf had no boulders to hide behind. That made it difficult in the darkness for anyone to try to sneak up, but it also made it dangerous for him to move down.

He crawled slowly and silently. If his plan worked, it might give them a chance. He shook his head. They didn't have a chance, and he knew it. All he could do was inflict as much pain as possible, kill as many of them as he could before they killed him.

Dave's plan was to hide himself away from the shelf, and when Scott's men rushed across the open ground, he'd blast them from behind. He was aware that once he opened fire, it would be easy to circle behind him, and he might not make it back.

Dave wiggled on his stomach and slowly squirmed among some jagged rocks off to one side of the shelf. The stars dimmed as the sky slowly began to lighten. He wouldn't have long to wait. He pressed his forehead against the cool rock and said a quick prayer.

When Scott ordered his men to open fire, the bullets whizzed by him. They struck the shelf, and Dave could tell from the sound that they were ricocheting dangerously inside the ledge.

He couldn't tell how many men were with Scott, but from the amount of firing going on, he figured it must be fifteen or twenty. There was no return fire from the shelf, and Dave only hoped Ted and Henrietta were still alive.

He peeked around a boulder and saw eight men advancing across the open ground. Scott was playing it safe; part of his group fired into the overhang, while others crossed the open ground. The men moved quickly and soon were past where he lay hidden.

Dave picked up his Henry. "By God, if I'm going to die, they'll know they were in a gunfight," he said to himself. And with that bitter proclamation, he opened fire.

It caught the gunmen by surprise. Before they had a chance to duck for cover, Dave killed four and narrowly missed two others.

Dave felt that he was safe from behind for a few moments, but he still glanced nervously over his shoulder to be certain.

The four men in front of him were now shielded by low rocks, and bullets pinned Dave down. Though it was impossible for him to get off any accurate shots, he blasted off four rounds blindly.

Suddenly a rifle sounded from the overhang, and Dave heard a scream. He now knew that there were only three outlaws in front of him.

A gunman leaped to his feet and started running away. Dave fired two shots, and the man crashed to the ground. Now only one gunman was left alive in front of him.

Two men had circled behind Dave, and one fired three shots that kicked up granite chips around his face. He grabbed his Adams and blasted off a shot in return. It missed.

Scott's men were over the shock of seeing the seven gunmen wiped out and were again firing heavily into the overhang and at him.

Another man appeared behind Dave. Dave blasted off two more shots. Missed again.

He grabbed his Henry and emptied his Adams at the two men behind him to pin them down for a moment. He leaped over rocks and dashed for the shelter of larger boulders twenty feet closer to the shelf. Scott's riflemen fired round after round at him as he dove behind the safety of a large outcropping. He was puffing heavily as he crawled around to the other side.

He fired three blind shots in the direction of the riflemen, but their bullets were kicking up so much dust and rock chips around him, he kept his head down and quickly reloaded his Henry.

A moment later, the rifle shots stopped coming toward him. Before he could figure out why, he heard a sound behind him. Dave twisted around and saw the last gunman smiling with grim satisfaction as he stood looking down at Dave.

The man never got to fire his revolver. A shot rang down from the shelf and flattened the gunman. Nor was that the only shot from the overhang. Scott's riflemen were pinned down from the rapid fire coming from the ledge.

Dave needed no second invitation. He grabbed the Henry and raced up the path for the shelf at top speed. Even with the steady cover from the shelf, Dave thought a rifleman would shoot him before he reached the safety of the ledge. He felt as if his legs had weights on them as he struggled up the narrow path, gasping and out of breath. Suddenly he heard the *click, click* of empty chambers. Whoever was firing the Henry from the shelf had run out of bullets. Dave still had ten long yards to go before he reached shelter. He was an open target, and he knew it. Any moment a bullet would smash into his back, and he'd be dead.

Unexpectedly, the sun's intense morning rays streaked over the top of the the cliff and momentarily blinded Scott's riflemen. Dave forced his aching legs to keep going, and he dove over the shelf barricade, amazed to be alive.

Henrietta was holding Ted up so he could shoot. The Henry slowly slipped from his hand and fell into his lap. He smiled weakly at Dave.

Dave quickly crawled over and helped Henrietta lay Ted back under the rock shelter.

With one finger Ted painfully drew something on Dave's chest.

Dave suddenly understood and grinned down at his badly wounded friend. "All right, so it was a dumb plan. They can't all be brilliant."

Ted rolled his eyes and smiled slightly.

Dave took Ted's hand, squeezed it gently, and said solemnly, "You can be my bodyguard anytime, Ted. And you can ride with me anywhere, anytime."

Ted closed his eyes but nodded that he understood.

Dave glanced at Henrietta and said gently, "You, too, Miss Byrne. Anywhere, anytime."

Tears rolled down her cheeks. "Was he scolding you?"

Dave smiled at her. "Yeah, for a fellow who can't talk, he sure manages to get in the last word most of the time."

Dave glanced at Ted and saw the flicker of a grin. "That's it, always taking a nap when there's work to be done."

But Ted didn't hear Dave's last remark. He was out cold again.

Dave stole a quick look over the barricade and shook his head. He reloaded all the guns. The firing had stopped, and Henrietta looked at him quizzically.

"They're working out a plan of attack," Dave explained. "This will be it. They'll pin us down. A few men will get across the open ground, and that will be it."

"We have no chance?" Henrietta asked. "No chance at all?"

Dave sighed quietly and shook his head. "Don't fire until I tell you to."

She nodded.

Dave looked at her with a special pride. She covered Ted with a blanket. The only tears she'd shed had been for Ted, not herself. The women in the Byrne family were really something.

Scott's men started firing. Dave peered out a small crevice in the barricade, waiting for the men to start across the open ground. Dave sensed the bullets as they screamed above his head and ricocheted off the rocks. His face and body were soon covered with small cuts from rock chips, but he didn't feel any pain. Henrietta placed herself beside Ted to protect him with her own body, watching for Dave to tell her to start firing.

Two men started across the open ground, but before they were halfway across, they were shot dead.

Dave's mouth twisted in puzzlement. He hadn't shot them. He couldn't tell if they'd been shot by their own men or what. The rifle firing stopped.

Dave's brow wrinkled into a frown. Henrietta scooted over and peeked out.

He mumbled to her, "Damnation. I don't have a clue what the hell is going on."

Dave didn't like the sound of this silence. When the gunfire started again, he ducked—until he realized the bullets weren't aimed at them. He peeked up over the rocks but still couldn't see anything.

"Damnation!" Dave exploded. "What the hell are they up to?"

Suddenly, a man rode full speed toward the shelf. Dave brought his Henry to his shoulder and aimed—but didn't fire.

Dave watched in wonder as Captain Slim Filmore leaped from his horse and raced up the path to the shelf. He dived over the rocky barricade and landed by Dave's feet.

Slim smiled broadly up at Dave and asked, "Everybody all right? You two look like hell."

Dave glanced at Henrietta and realized that her face and arms were covered with blood from scratches and cuts from all the rock ricocheting around. He figured he must look just as bad. He motioned to Ted and said hoarsely, "Ted's been shot, bad."

Slim checked Ted's bandages and whistled softly. He explained, "We don't have a doctor with us."

"There's a doctor in the valley if we can get to him before Scott does."

Slim said firmly, "Well, we've got them boxed in—"

A loud explosion never allowed Slim to finish his statement. "Good Lord!" he exclaimed.

"Blasting oil!" Dave shouted. "Miss Byrne, give Slim here Ted's Henry."

She tossed the rifle to Slim as Dave raced down to his horse; Slim followed close behind. Dave quickly tightened the saddle on Chocolate, and they rode rapidly to a small ridge.

Another trooper rode up. "Captain, they threw something at us, and it exploded like I've never seen before. Killed one of our horses and injured Private Leach and Private Vegas."

"How bad are they hurt?"

"Not too badly, sir, but they can't ride."

"How many got away?" Slim asked.

"About five or six, as best as I could tell, sir. We killed the rest."

Slim nodded and asked the trooper, "Can the men walk?"

"Yes, probably."

"Good. You tell them to go up to that shelf back there"—Slim pointed it out—"and make sure nothing happens to the woman and wounded man there. We'll send a doctor and wagon back for all of them as soon as we can."

The trooper nodded and asked Dave, "Did you do that?" He pointed to the bodies lying in front of the overhang.

"With some help from my friends."

The trooper nodded in admiration.

Dave turned to Slim. "Where the hell did you come from?"

"We were less than a half day on the road to Fort Smith when a company of troops from there rode up to meet us. They had gotten word we were in trouble. They'd already come upon a group of Scott's men setting up an ambush for us. Of course, they weren't expecting anyone coming from the north, so the troops managed to wipe out six and take two prisoners.

"We turned around with the company to come here but stopped in Livermore for provisions. That's where we found out about Blackfoot. Jim stayed behind to gather information, but I decided I'd better get right up here and not wait for more troops. We really pushed it hard."

Dave nodded. "That's the only reason we're alive right now."

"Good to be able to repay a debt." Slim grinned.

"Did you see Jamie's daughter?"

"She's gone. Nobody's seen her." Slim paused. "Maybe Scott's got her."

Dave nodded. "I hope not."

They rode quickly to where the troops had fought Scott. An ugly, blackened hole in the ground marked all too plainly where the blasting oil had been thrown. A sergeant hurried to Slim and said quickly, "We killed eight of them, sir, but at least six got away. Are we going after them?"

Slim turned to Dave and asked, "What do you think?"

Dave was silent for a moment. "Slim, if we don't hit them today, right now, while they're running, they'll regroup. We'd be back where we started. They'll probably go back to their headquarters. It could be rough getting in, but I think we should try it."

Slim turned to the sergeant and said, "Have the men mount up, Sergeant." Slim added to Dave, "I don't think we can push the horses much more. They're about worn out."

Dave studied the condition of the mounts and agreed. "Yeah, that could be a problem. Have your men ride the horses Scott's men left behind. You can bring your horses down when we come back for Ted and your wounded."

"Good idea." Slim directed the sergeant to get the men onto the fresher horses.

Dave asked, "Are your men up to this?"

"They're up to it," Slim stated firmly. "They saw the bodies of their comrades and the major, and they've heard about the ambush. They're up to it."

Shortly before noon, they reached the Bowman Fort. Dave

saw no sign of activity on top of the stockade fence. He didn't want the troopers rushing the fence and getting picked off one by one, so he decided to investigate alone. He ran out of the woods and up to the fence. The three loose logs were fastened in place. There would be no hole to slip through this time.

He squinted through a crack in the fence. Nothing moved inside. He waved for Slim and the troopers. They hurried over to him with the ladder he'd hidden when he came to rescue Henrietta.

Dave was the first to go up. The ranch was still, but not with the stillness of a trap. The troops rushed over the fence and spread out while Dave tried to figure out what Scott had done.

Slim came up to Dave and asked, "What do you think?"

"I'm afraid," Dave said angrily, "that he's outmaneuvered us." He slapped his hat against one leg in anger. "Ask someone to check that low building over there and see if the doctor is in it."

Slim decided to do it himself.

A corporal ran up to Dave and said, "There's a lot of ammunition in a small building on the other side of the house."

"Good." Dave nodded. "Check with Captain Filmore and see if he wants to load it into a wagon or leave it here under guard."

Dave did a double take when he watched several men and women and three children walk out of the low building. Dave saw Slim talking to Dr. Zimms and hurried over. "You have to get to Ted right away."

"Right. I was just telling him about Ted," Slim said.

Dr. Zimms stared at Dave for a long moment and said, "David? David Kramer, is that really you under all that dirt and blood?"

"It's me, Doc. Bruised and battered but still ticking." He reached out and shook the doctor's hand warmly.

The doctor shook his head. "Why, I just don't believe—"

"David!"

Dave froze when he heard his name, then spun around to where the voice had come from. "Dad!"

They ran to each another, threw their arms around each other, and hugged warmly.

"David, David," his father cried. "I . . . just . . ." He tried to hold back his emotion but couldn't. "Are you all right?" He held

Dave out at arm's length. "You're covered in blood, and you have cuts all over your face."

"I've been in a bit of a gunfight, but I'm fine. These are all just nicks."

Dr. Zimms slapped Dave's father on the back and exclaimed, "The captain says it's been David causing all this trouble for Scott."

"Is that right?" his father asked, wiping tears from his cheeks. Dave nodded.

"You did a fine job, David," Zimms proclaimed. "All I've been doing lately is pulling your bullets out of Scott's men." He smiled and added, "Those we didn't bury."

Dave said, "Slim, I want you to meet my father, Robert Kramer. I thought he was dead."

"Well, hi, Mr. Kramer. This is a fine surprise."

"For everyone, Captain. For everyone."

Dave suddenly had a thought. "The Byrne family," he said aloud.

His father asked, "What's that?"

"I'm sorry, Dad, I can't explain now. Slim, I need some men. I think I know where Scott is."

" 'Some,' hell. I'll put the sergeant in charge here, and we can take off together."

Dave turned to his father. "Dad, I wish I could talk to you, but there's a family here in the valley who may be in a heap of trouble."

"The Byrnes. We know about them and the girl Scott was holding. Was that you that rescued her?"

"Yup."

"Well done, David. We have much to talk about, but it can wait. Do what you have to do. We can talk later. Zimms here tells me that a friend of yours is hurt up in the hills. I'll go along and help out."

Dave smiled warmly at his father and said, "Treat him with care. He's special. He's saved my life more than once. Byrne's daughter Henrietta is with him." He started to turn away, stopped, and added, "They're both like family, Dad."

His father nodded that he understood.

Slim split up his men; three would go with Dr. Zimms and Dave's father in a wagon, so they could bring Ted and the two wounded soldiers back. Some would stay at the Bowman fort to protect the ammunition and the civilians they'd released. The rest would go with Dave and Slim.

Dave's emotions were a jumble—exuberance that his father was alive and well, fear for the Byrne family, especially Julie, and worry about Ted. Slim's shout snapped him out of his thoughts.

"Smoke over there!" Slim pointed, and Dave knew the smoke came from the Byrne house.

They pushed their tired horses on. As they came closer, Dave knew his fears were correct. The Byrne house was ablaze. When they rode up, three men lay dead in front of the house, and one was Ralph Byrne. Mrs. Byrne was off to one side, lying in a pool of blood. Dave hurried over to her, knelt, and softly called her name.

"Mrs. Byrne, it's Dave Kramer."

She opened her eyes, but they were glazed and did not see. She'd been shot in the stomach and chest, and her hands were covered with blood as she tried to hold back her death. She touched her lips with her tongue and begged, "Water . . . please, some water." Her voice cracked.

A trooper handed Dave his canteen. Dave tilted it up carefully to her lips. She took a sip.

"Ralph fought them, Mr. Kramer. My man fought them." She looked around wildly. "They took Julie . . . they took my Julie . . . did you save Henrietta?"

"Yes, she's safe and fine."

"Henrietta is safe. God bless you. Take care of my baby, Mr. Kramer. Take care of my baby."

"Where is he?" Dave asked.

"I hid him . . . under the bed." Her weak voice pleaded with him. "Please, take care of him."

Dave looked up at the house slowly collapsing, flames stretching into the sky, and said in a whisper, "I'll try."

Mrs. Byrne didn't hear. Dave gently closed her eyelids, laid her back on the ground, and stood wearily.

One of the troopers pointed at the house and asked Dave, "Was her baby in there?"

"Yes." Dave turned away from the trooper with tears on his face.

The trooper took two hesitant steps toward the house and then slowly turned away.

Slim watched the proceedings quietly. He sent some of his men to dig graves. Then he walked over to Dave.

Dave glanced at him and in a husky voice said, "They've taken the daughter, Julie, as a hostage."

Slim nodded. "We'll let the horses rest and have the men eat. We'll get them. My hunch is, they realize they've been beaten and will try to make a run for it. Since they don't know about the back pass, they'll head out the front. Before we came through the pass, I sent a detachment of men to block it off."

A small look of hope spread over Dave's face.

Slim continued. "The detachment is green. So is the lieutenant. But they may be able to slow him down. Our horses will be in better shape than Scott's, so . . ." He shrugged uncertainly.

Dave put an arm around Slim's shoulders and said, "You ought to be a general."

Slim gazed at the carnage in front of him and said bitterly, "Not quite." He sighed softly. "You try to eat some food. We still have a long way to go."

Dave nodded and walked to the fire where coffee was heating.

He took the coffee, hardtack, and dried beef that was handed to him with a nod of thanks and glanced at the graves being dug. He stared at them for a long time. Finally, his eyes lifted to the sky, he said quietly, "Lord, if he hurts Julie, I'll hunt him down and kill him. I'll have to, Lord. I'll just have to."

He sat on a log and ate without tasting the food.

Chapter Twelve

The road out of Quiet Valley ran through a series of twists and turns past granite boulders and high mountains on either side as it approached the pass. Then the mountain ridges gradually spread into a long funnel two miles across, flattened, and flowed into a rolling prairie that stretched to the horizon.

The long, thin rays of the sun blended into evening shadows as Slim, Dave, and the troopers approached the start of the long series of turns in the road before it opened into the pass.

Slim signaled the troops to halt. He straightened in his saddle, balanced himself in the stirrups, stood, and looked for signs of his men. His face squeezed into a tight frown. "They should be around here. I don't like this."

Dave nodded. "I expect Scott made a run for it, got through, and they gave chase."

"Maybe . . . maybe." Slim looked worried. "That detachment was green. All of them so young."

They followed the road into the twisting series of turns past granite outcroppings. Dave rode ahead, intently watching the road. Finally, he saw what he was looking for—some clear tracks that told a story.

He dismounted and explained to Slim, "So many tracks coming and going, it's hard to get a reading. I figure the wagon tracks over on that side of the road are from when Scott brought the ammo wagon back. But these tracks here"—Dave pointed at the road—"are recent. Scott came down this road fast on the right, then veered over to the trail here." He pointed to more hoofprints. "He must have spotted your men, but your troops must have figured that he had to cut in here and damn near stopped him by cutting back to the road first. Your lieutenant did that well."

Dave quickly remounted Chocolate, and they raced down the twisting path. Slim yelled at Dave, but he saw it at the same time. A cold chill ran through Dave.

The troopers who had tried to block Scott's escape from the valley stood quietly by their horses. One young officer knelt by a woman. A dead horse lay on the ground.

Dave swung down from his saddle as Chocolate skidded to a stop, and he ran to the woman.

Julie Byrne spoke with pain and fear in her voice. "I . . . I hurt so much."

Dave fell to his knees beside her. "It's all right. I'm here." He glanced at the lieutenant. The lieutenant shook his head and lifted the bandages covering her stomach. "The shot hit her in the back, and the bullet came out the front."

"How did it happen?" Dave asked bitterly.

The lieutenant explained. "They ran through us at the entrance, eight of them. We were close behind—almost cut them off. Jordan shot one of their horses. They pulled up in the rocks over there and made a fight of it for a while. We killed two of them. Finally the leader said they'd give us the woman in exchange for a chance to escape, or they'd kill her.

"I said I'd do it, and this tall, ugly man rode up with her. He dropped her from his horse, and after he got far enough away, he turned and shot her in the back."

Dave nodded and gently stroked Julie's white face.

She said in a whisper, "He's killed us all."

Dave shook his head. "Not all. Henrietta's safe."

She smiled painfully. "Oh, I'm so glad. Take care of her, won't you?" Her gaze moved to the lieutenant, and she said painfully, "Thank you for trying to help me."

The lieutenant's emotions only allowed him to nod.

She tried to say something to Dave, but a wave of pain jerked her body, and she fainted away.

The lieutenant said to Dave, "I did what I could, but the shot did such terrible damage."

"Yeah," Dave mumbled. "Yeah, I know."

Dave and the lieutenant sat on either side of Julie, neither of them speaking.

The men prepared camp for the night, but there was no talk. They mostly sat and watched Dave, the lieutenant, and the woman.

One recruit sniffed hard and nodded at Slim. "I'm sorry, Captain."

"I know, Jordan. We all are."

Dave felt Julie's hand tighten, then slowly relax. He sighed tiredly and nodded to the lieutenant. Together they stood. The lieutenant looked down at Julie's face and said, "It's just not right."

Dave went to his horse and mounted. He said to Slim, "I'm going to take her back and bury her with her family."

Slim nodded. "You want us to come with you?"

Dave shook his head. He had to do this alone.

Slim rested a hand on Dave's arm, "If you need someone to talk to later . . ."

Dave nodded wearily.

Two troopers lifted Julie to him.

He rode through the darkness carrying her in his arms. The Byrne home still burned when he arrived. The wind occasionally stirred up the embers and showered them up into the sky with a puff.

Dave dug a grave for Julie beside her mother and father. He dug ferociously in the hard soil like a man gone mad. He dug with anger, with hate, with bitterness, but even when he finished, the poison still churned inside him.

He stood over her grave for a long time. He hadn't even gotten to know her. Just spent a few special moments with her. Abruptly, he tipped his head back and yelled a long, savage sound of pain and fury. He buckled over with his hands on his knees and gulped deep breaths of air as he stared at Julie's grave. A feral, vicious, inhuman sound exploded from his mouth, again and again, until no more sound would come.

The ride back to the Bowman fort was long and cold in the darkness. Dave drew his thin jacket close around his neck and held it with his left hand.

The guards halted him when he approached, but when they recognized him, they waved him in. They asked about Scott, but Dave shook his head without speaking.

He went into the main house and up to the top bedroom. He figured they'd take Ted there. He was right.

Dr. Zimms heard him coming up the stairs and met him in the hallway. "My God, are you all right?"

Dave's pale, blood-streaked face radiated his pain and rage.

Dave found that he could only talk in a whisper. "I'm all right. I lost some good friends today."

Zimms said quietly, "I'm terribly sorry, David."

"How's Ted?"

"It's too early to tell. The wounds were bad. I've removed the bullets. He's in a stupor. If he comes out of it, he'll have a chance."

"And if he doesn't?" Dave asked hoarsely.

Zimms silently shook his head.

Dave glanced into the room at Ted. Henrietta dozed in a rocking chair by the bed.

"Henrietta's parents, her baby brother, her sister Julie—all killed by Scott," Dave whispered.

Zimms' eyes closed. "There's been so much death in this valley." He studied Henrietta thoughtfully. "She's a strong and special woman. You go get some rest. I'll tell her when she wakes up."

Dave nodded tiredly. He was weary of death. He walked back down the stairs and sat on a bench and stared at the wall across from him. He wanted to kick something, to beat something with his fists, but he closed his eyes and leaned his head back in bitter realization that there was nothing he could do.

When he opened his eyes again, he realized that the sun was up and that he must have fallen asleep. He was stretched out on the bench. A blanket covered him, and he wondered who'd put it over him. Sitting up, he discovered someone had also taken off his boots. He stood stiffly and stretched to try to loosen up.

Jim Bates walked in with two cups of steaming coffee and handed one to Dave.

"Starting to think you weren't ever going to get up." Jim hesitated. "I'm sorry about the Byrne family."

"Thanks," Dave whispered in a grating voice.

"You know about Jamie?"

"Yeah, I know." Dave took a careful sip of the hot coffee and asked, "Where'd you come from? What time is it, anyway?" He sat back down and pulled on his boots.

Jim glanced at his pocket watch and said, "Ten-thirty. Slim rode in some time ago, so I'm pretty well filled in on what happened. You going after Scott?"

"Yeah. Got to."

Jim nodded. "I figured you would, so I had these made up for you." He handed some papers to Dave. "It's identification. You're officially on special assignment for the U.S. government, Major, and also a special agent for Wells Fargo. It's good to have friends in high places. Depending on where you are, one or the other should help. You're on salary, and if you find the stolen gold, you'll get ten percent of what you recover."

Dave looked down at the papers and then slowly pushed them down inside his shirt pocket. "Thanks, I—"

"Hell," Jim interrupted, "don't make a speech. I just wish I could go with you." He paused for a moment. "I miss my brother, Dave. That last night he made a bad mistake, but he was a good man, and he served his country with honor." Jim sighed. "He was a fine older brother."

"He was just doing what he thought was right," Dave said hoarsely. "No one can fault him for that. No man deserves to be ambushed."

"Thanks for those words."

"Jim, I'm not going to bring Scott back."

Jim studied Dave intently, trying to be sure he understood what Dave was saying. He took a sip of coffee and then nodded in agreement. "Good."

Dave leaned his head back against the wall. The pain inside ate at him.

"I've more bad news for you."

Dave asked quickly, "Not Ted?"

"No, no, I'm sorry. I'd forgotten about your friend, Ted. He's still in a coma, no change. No, this is about Sally Blackfoot."

"She dead too?"

"No, but maybe worse. The night Jamie was killed, she bought an old, used covered wagon with two mules and left town. One of the Indian scouts with the troop tracked her and said that she met with a large group of riders moving with a heavy wagon."

"You're thinking it might have been Scott, with the stolen ammo wagon?" Dave questioned.

"It crossed my mind. They met in an area where there isn't much wagon traffic and late at night. Very strange."

"Did the scout see them meet or only read the signs?" Dave asked.

"Just the signs. I didn't find out about Jamie and Sally until the day after he was murdered. I sent my scout out to track Sally after things weren't making any sense. I thought she might have been kidnapped, but that didn't seem to be the case. The odd part is, she left town before Jamie was killed. At least a couple of hours before."

"Why would she leave when her father was so badly hurt, unless she was forced?"

"Exactly," Jim said. "That was my first thought, but some people saw her go, and she was alone. No one was forcing her to go."

"So where was she going?" Dave asked.

"I wish I knew. And who'd she meet up with? If she met up with Scott, why did he just let her go on? That's not like him." Jim shook his head at his own questions. "Or was the meeting planned?"

"That doesn't make any sense," Dave said, frowning. "Did the scout figure out what happened next?"

"She turned and headed toward the foothills by herself. The riders and wagon headed here, to Quiet Valley." Jim asked, "Do you remember asking me back at the fort if I thought anyone could have overheard us in Jamie's room at the Golden Spur? You said it was as though Scott knew our plans before we did. You don't suppose it could have been Sally, do you?"

Dave's head snapped toward Jim in shock. "Damnation, Jim, I don't want to think that. Not her own father."

"Nor I. I suspect we will never know, but there are some big questions I'd surely like to know the answers to."

Dave pondered what Jim had said while they walked into the kitchen. Slim and Dave's father were at the table, looking at a map.

"I think he's heading for Kansas," Slim said. "There's six of them left, as best we can figure. We rounded up eight more in the valley. There may be a few more, but we'll get them. Scott himself is the main problem now."

Dave ate quietly while the men talked. Dave's father explained that Ted and Henrietta would be staying with him while Ted recovered. Dave knew Ted might never wake from his coma, but he didn't speak his dark thoughts.

After eating, he went up to Ted's room. Henrietta sat by Ted's still body, but she stood when Dave entered the room. She still had many cuts on her face from yesterday's battle, and her eyes were red from lack of sleep and crying.

"The doctor is getting some rest. We won't know anything until Teddy comes out of his coma."

Dave put his arm around her and hugged her gently. "Did Zimms talk to you? Did he tell you—?"

"I know." Tears flowed into Henrietta's eyes, but she refused to lose control. "I already miss them so much."

"I want you to know that you and Ted are part of *my* family now."

Henrietta smiled sadly at him. "Your father told me the same thing this morning. Now I know where you get that kind, caring quality." She sighed and asked, "Are you going after Scott?"

"I have to."

Henrietta reached up and kissed him on the cheek. "Come back to us. Don't let him kill you too."

Dave nodded and left the room.

Jim Bates, Slim, and Dave's father all walked out with him to the stable. Someone had saddled Chocolate and packed his gear for him.

Dave patted Chocolate gently and mounted.

Jim reached into his pocket and handed a leather money pouch to Dave. Dave shook his head, but Jim shook his in return and explained, "It's not my money. You've been on the Wells Fargo payroll since I met you with Jamie. There's gold and silver coins. No scrip. Wire me if you need help or more money."

Dave leaned down and shook Jim's hand warmly.

Dave's father smiled up at him, "Your cause is just, David." He patted Dave on the leg. "Take care, and hurry home to us."

"Be safe, Major," Slim said, saluting Dave.

Dave lifted the brim of his hat and pulled it down firmly over his forehead in a return salute. He rode off without looking back.

Chapter Thirteen

Scott and his men moved slowly east. Dave couldn't understand why they were going so slowly, but he was determined to take advantage of it. He pushed Chocolate hard that first week.

On the ninth day, shortly before noon, he spotted the six riders he sought far in the distance. Before he could ride within rifle range, they saw him and rapidly rode out of sight. Dave now realized why Scott had been riding slowly. He wanted to keep his horses fresh. It was a good plan.

Dave knew Chocolate was too tired to race after them. He eased her into a ground-covering trot. After some time he dismounted, switched into his moccasins, and ran beside her—another trick Jamie had taught him. It stretched his legs and kept his endurance up, and it gave Chocolate a break from carrying him. Chocolate was the key to his success. He couldn't afford to wear her out, so throughout the rest of the day he alternated riding and running.

They were ahead of him, but not by much. Dave smiled grimly. He felt a strange calm now that he knew for sure he was on their trail.

Scott and his men, realizing they were being followed, pushed their horses, but no matter how fast they rode, or how far, Dave stayed on their trail. He had to control his impatience and concentrate on keeping the pressure on Scott and his men. They were staying off the main roads, attempting to hide their trail, but without any luck.

The high-plains country was lush grassland, with rolling hills, scarce trees, and few places to hide. When Dave scanned the distant landscape, he could sometimes see Scott and his men far ahead of him, but they could also see him.

After the second week, a bone-deep numbness settled into Dave. He felt a constant tension that never allowed him to relax, the sense of an endless journey that had been going on forever.

He kept thinking Scott would turn south, head for Texas and then down into Mexico, but the trail continued east. Scott's plan puzzled Dave and made him uneasy.

Late that night Dave smelled food. He rode up over a ridge and saw that he was only a mile from Scott's men. They saw him too, and Dave rode into the camp to find only a weak stew still swinging on a green branch above a small fire.

He hadn't eaten a hot meal since he left the fort. Sitting on the ground and hungrily spooning the hot, watery liquid into his mouth, he laughed—a hard, bitter laugh. Scott was running from Dave as a man would from a hellhound.

Dave remained continuously alert for an ambush, slowing whenever he traveled through dangerous terrain. As the days wore on, however, the burning hate smoldering within him pushed him even harder.

On day sixteen, early in the morning, the sky turned an ominous gray. On and off during the day it rained, sometimes quite hard, more often just a misty sprinkle that kept him constantly damp. The sky growled and grumbled its warning of worse to come. Dave's poncho gave him some protection, but the rain was cold, and even with all his gear on, he couldn't stay warm.

Near the end of the gloomy afternoon, the clouds turned from gray to black. A strange darkness cloaked the land and made Dave uneasy.

The first crashes of thunder were so loud and sudden that Chocolate bolted forward in terror, almost unseating Dave. Dave's horsemanship was all that prevented him from being thrown. Chocolate danced nervously, but Dave quieted her down gently yet firmly.

Lightning flashed over the sky, followed by booming thunderclaps. Rain poured down. It felt like standing under a waterfall. The trail turned into a river of running water and mud.

Twice they were almost caught in flash floods that tore through narrow canyons, sweeping away everything that wasn't rooted down. Twice Chocolate fought for footing while she narrowly carried herself and Dave away from a watery death. All but blinded by the fury of the storm, he continued in what he hoped was the correct direction.

Against the downpour, his poncho stuck to his body and made his clothes icy cold. The cold sank into his soul, and where the poncho didn't cover his pant legs, the wetness turned his legs into human icicles. The trail, or what he hoped was the trail, was a river of flowing mud intermixed with branches, rocks, and anything loose. Chocolate fought for purchase.

Dave dismounted to allow Chocolate better footing without his weight. As he stepped down, he sank deeply into the brown muck.

Horse and man struggled forward. The watery goo held each footstep, twice sucking Dave out of one of his boots. He'd stop, pull his boot out of the mud, pour the muck out, and shove his foot back into the cold, wet boot. He tried going barefoot, but the cold water quickly made his feet numb.

When night came, it came suddenly and with an intense darkness that wiped out Dave's ability to see things even directly in front of him. He looked for shelter, but there was none. With no horizon or stars to take a bearing on, he groped his way forward, tripping on rocks and bumping or crashing into bushes.

Even Chocolate's usually reliable sense of direction was not working in this darkness. Only the occasional flashes of lightning gave Dave a sense of where they were going.

Then he saw a light.

He stopped and blinked to be sure he wasn't seeing some rainy mirage. But it was a light. So tiny at first that, for a moment, Dave thought it might be a star low on the horizon. But he knew that couldn't be, since rain still flowed from the sky.

He almost called out, partly for joy and partly in relief at something to form a bearing on. However, a sense of danger warned him not to give away his position until he knew more.

As he approached the light, he saw Scott and his men huddled around a small fire under a rock shelter.

Dave pulled the Henry from its sheath. He stepped down from Chocolate into thick, oozing mud. Slowly he moved stealthily toward the outlaws, trying hard to not step out of his boots as the slimy mud impeded each step.

The rain and thunder hid his movement, but twenty yards away, a bolt of lightning struck a small tree on a rise behind him. When the men looked up, they saw his silhouette.

Everybody started firing at once. Realizing that they were open targets by the fire, Scott and his men raced for their horses and soon were absorbed by the rain and the darkness. Dave glared with disgust at the blackness that hid their escape. He hadn't hit one of them. He sighed and lowered his head. The rain poured off his hat brim. Of course, they hadn't hit him either. A slow grin formed on his face. He shrugged and returned to Chocolate and led her under the rock shelter.

There, out of the storm, he stripped off her saddle and bridle. He was so tired he could hardly move, but he finished caring for Chocolate before he sat by the fire.

The small blaze had warmed up the cave. Sitting exhausted beside the fire, he slowly pulled off his wet clothes. He grunted and groaned as he struggled to tug off his wet boots. He wrung out his socks and placed them on sticks in front of the fire. The darkness surrounded him in a protective black shelter. His weariness warred with his judgment. He was an easy target, but he didn't care. Leaning back against a rock warmed by the fire, he pulled his damp blanket around his body and closed his eyes for a moment.

He woke with a start, not sure where he was. He could tell from the light that it was midmorning, but where was he? Then he remembered. He jumped to his feet, cursing himself for his stupidity and at the same time amazed to discover he was still alive.

A flat, low, white mist hugged the ground and gave him the feeling he was looking down on the plain from a high mountain. The ground was soaked, the dark sky just resting before it would start to pour again, but there was no rain at the moment. His clothes were dry. He stoked the fire, dressed, and took the time to fix a hot breakfast with coffee. He was dry and rested, but he knew Scott and his men had to be wet and tired. That thought pleased him.

Days later Dave rode into Abilene. He guessed that he'd been riding for four weeks or more. The last week, he'd ridden through three storms, one after the other. Any hopes of tracking Scott were lost in a running river of mud and ooze. Hoofprints were gone almost the moment they were made.

He was covered with weeks of mud, sweat, and beard, his eyes sunk deep within his face. Chocolate was near exhaustion and trudged forward with her head down.

For the first time in days, there were only overcast skies and no rain. He crossed Mud Creek into Abilene and smiled wryly at the appropriateness of the creek's name on the crude sign. Abiline's main street was as muddy as the trail Dave had been trying to follow. It was a town of crude log huts. Dave turned Chocolate in to a small blacksmith shop and stable.

A short, thickset man with muscular arms and a peg leg and wearing a Confederate cap hobbled up to him. The blacksmith stared at Dave with a mixture of fascination and apprehension.

Dave stepped down stiffly from Chocolate and surveyed the two other horses in the corral. Satisfied that the animals did not belong to Scott's men, he drew a coin from his damp pocket, flipped it to the man, and said, "The very best for this horse. Wash her down with warm water, and dry her carefully. Then oats, hay, water, and your warmest stall." Dave glared at the man.

The blacksmith stood mesmerized by this exhausted, hard-looking rider covered with mud. He held Dave's coin in his hand, seemingly without knowing he held it.

When he hesitated, Dave growled, "Did you hear me?"

The man jumped and said, "Yes—yes, sir. Sorry, sir. I'll take fine care of her."

Dave pulled his gear off and walked tiredly up the street. He carried his Henry in his left hand, his saddlebag over his right shoulder. He stopped a passerby and asked where he could get something to eat.

The man pointed up the street to a small log structure with a crude BUTTERFIELD OVERLAND STAGE sign in front of it He seemed glad that he was going in the opposite direction.

An old woman, her gray hair pulled back tightly, wrinkled her brow when Dave walked in. She seemed to smell trouble riding on the shoulders of this hard, dirty man and wanted none of it in her place.

Dave sat on a bench with his back against a wall and stared down the few customers who glanced nervously at him. The woman walked over to him and said firmly, "Don't want no trouble here, sir. I'd appre—"

Dave didn't let her finish. "Don't *sir* me, just bring me food. Lots of it. Steak, eggs, potatoes, coffee, pie, and anything else you've got. Move!"

She pushed out her lower lip at this stranger who kept his eyes on the door and seemed to consider telling him to leave. But when his muddy, hate-filled eyes met hers, she scurried out to the kitchen.

Dave had just finished his meal when he heard the sound of the one-legged blacksmith outside the eatery. A face popped around the front door, peered in, then withdrew. Shortly after, a hard-faced man and two others armed with shotguns walked in. The other customers quickly left.

The hard-faced man walked to Dave's table, but before he could say anything, Dave shoved a chair out for him with one foot. One man had swung his shotgun up at the move but then let it drop with embarrassment.

The man sat down easily, loosely. "We don't have any law here yet, so sometimes we have to make do."

Dave nodded. He volunteered the information he knew this man was after. "Name's Dave Kramer from Quiet Valley, Colorado Territory. I'm after a killer called Jedd Scott who's on the run with six men. Scott's an ugly, tall, skinny bastard. Dresses in black like an undertaker and smokes thin cigars. I've been tracking him for weeks." He threw the credentials Jim Bates had given him onto the table.

The man picked up the credentials and glanced at them. He eased back in his chair and waved his friends off. "I'm Charley

Thompson. I just got word about you a few days ago. Some surveyors from the Kansas Pacific Railway told me about you. You covered plenty of ground in this weather to show up here so soon."

"The damnable thing is, that bastard is always just ahead of me. Almost had him once, but he's tough. Damn tough."

Charley nodded slowly. "Well, in fact, I'm pretty sure his gang did pass through here last night."

Dave put down his coffee cup and asked, "You don't think he laid over?"

"I don't think so. But he killed a farmer and his wife. Stole four old whey-bellies and supplies. A nasty job. I didn't learn of it until this morning."

Dave leaned back and sighed. "Damnation, my fault. I've been pushing him hard. Otherwise I don't think he'd have risked a killing here."

"Perhaps, but a gang like that gets in the habit of killing. Sometimes they don't know how to stop."

"Which direction?" Dave asked.

"Looks as though they turned south, heading down toward the Santa Fe Trail. We tried to follow them but lost their trail in the mud. This damn rain makes it almost impossible to track anyone."

Dave nodded sadly. He understood that.

"Townsfolk were afraid you might be part of the gang."

"Yeah, I guess I do look off my feed."

"We heard this man did some bad things. Quiet Valley is a long ways from here. Why'd he head east anyway after what he did?" Charley asked.

"I can't figure that out. It doesn't make any sense, him heading east and all. I thought he'd try to go down into the Territory of New Mexico or Texas and then maybe over into Mexico."

"Maybe he thought that's what you'd think and tried to fool you by heading east. Maybe he figured you'd go south and then give up when you didn't find him. He'd go east a ways, then drop south when he figured it was safe."

"Well," Dave said thoughtfully, "if that was his plan, he learned quick enough that it didn't work."

"You going to bring him back for trial?"

Dave looked long and hard at Charley Thompson and said harshly, "Sir, if I ever get close enough to him, I'm going to kill him."

He collected his papers, placed some coins on the table for the meal, then pulled his hat down low on his head and walked out of the restaurant.

The old woman came up to Charley and said, "I wouldn't want to be the one he's after."

Thompson nodded silently. He'd been thinking the same thing.

Dave trudged slowly up the muddy street, his shoulders slumped with fatigue. He was sick about what Charley Thompson had told him. Another innocent man and woman killed by the Undertaker. He couldn't help feeling responsible. He noticed a sign that read FRONTIER STORE & SALOON and headed for it.

Two steps inside the saloon, still preoccupied with his thoughts, he realized something was wrong. It was a mistake he seldom made. Before he could rectify it, a bullet smashed into him and took him down to the floor. The Henry slid from his hand. He painfully pulled his Adams.

From the looks on their faces, Scott and his men were as surprised to see Dave as he was to see them.

A shotgun exploded and blew a large hole in the wall above Dave's head. He tried to stand, but two more bullets smashed into his body. But he still held his Adams. Scott and his men headed for a side door. Dave painfully pulled the hammer back with both hands and fired at the last man trying to leave. The bullet tore into the man's back, hurling him out the door, dead.

Dave half crawled, half rolled out the front door. He tried again to get up but crashed to the muddy street. He lay on his side and glared down at his leg. He watched the blood ooze from a hole in his thigh without feeling the pain.

Scott and his men rode hard around the corner of the building. With shaking hands, Dave raised his Adams, pulled back the hammer, and tried to aim with blurring eyes. His shot was low. It hit Scott's horse. Horse and rider skidded in the mud.

Dave tried to pull back the hammer again but didn't have the strength. Through blurred, pain-filled eyes, he watched another rider help Scott onto the back of his horse. He heard a shotgun—Charley Thompson's?—firing at the gang, but . . .

Chapter Fourteen

Dave tried to pull himself up out of the darkness. The first sensation he felt was of heat, then pain—a slow, rolling, nerve-screaming pain. He tried to roll away from the hurt, but hands, strong hands, held him firmly. He tried to see, but only patches of light came and then faded.

Then he felt something gouging into his body, probing, hunting, scratching, and then horrible, excruciating pain. Darkness came back to his soul as he realized someone was probing for the slugs still embedded deep in his flesh.

When he woke again, the sky outside was dark. A man came in, and Dave thought he must be very old. He had a huge white beard, and his hair was long and white. Not until the man came closer to the bed did Dave realize that his hair was just prematurely white.

The man lifted the blanket and studied a bandage. He looked at Dave and said brashly, "Awake, huh? Good. You're damn lucky, boy. Damn lucky. Next time you decide to get gunned down, take a bath. You stank like hell when they brought you to me."

Dave nodded his head painfully, trying to wet his dry, chapped lips with his tongue. "Sorry about that." He said the words slowly and in a gravelly whisper. His throat ached. "I'll plan better next time."

"You don't have any idea how lucky you were *this* time. Abilene doesn't even have a doctor. I arrived on the stage to Denver a few minutes after you were shot, and this Thompson guy pulled me off to take care of you. You'd be talking to your maker now if I hadn't arrived. As I said, you are damn lucky, boy."

"Thanks. I'll remember next time I get shot. Make sure I'm clean and that you are close by on a stage. And your name?"

The doctor finally smiled and nodded. "Still got your sense of humor, huh? Good. You'll need that to help you heal. I'm Dr. Eric. Man outside has been waiting to see you. He says his name is Jim Bates. You up to talking to him?"

"Yeah!" Dave looked surprised. "How long have I been out?"

The doctor said over his shoulder as he walked out, "Four days."

Dave gasped hoarsely. "Damnation! Four days?"

Jim hurried in, and Dave whispered, "What are you doing here? I thought Wells Fargo was out in San Francisco."

"Yesterday, we were. Who knows where we'll be a year from now. One of my jobs is to check out the competition. We're a growing company." He shook his head at Dave. "You look like hell. You could use some good news. Ted's out of his coma. Still too early to tell if he's going to make it, but Zimms says his chances are better now."

"Ah." Dave smiled painfully. "That is good news."

"What about Jamie's daughter?"

"That news you're not going to like. I think we both sensed it. Scott and she are old friends, lovers of some sort. He convinced her to take the stolen gold to Mexico. Still a bunch we don't know, but the government gold *and* the spy were under our noses all the time."

"Good Lord," Dave mumbled. "She betrayed Jamie." He closed his eyes and said softly, "Her own father."

"I'd say that's how it happened." Jim shook his head. "Apparently, Scott didn't have as much faith in his plan to build an empire as we thought. Or perhaps he was afraid to trust his own men with that much money around. Why he'd trust Sally with it, I sure don't know."

Dave opened his eyes, grimaced from another wave of pain, and said in a whisper, "I still can't believe she'd let them gun down Jamie like that. How could she allow that to happen to her own father?"

"I don't know. But I imagine she's going to meet Scott somewhere along the border or in Mexico. Maybe even head for California."

"Maybe that's why he headed east, so I wouldn't overtake *her*. Give her plenty of time to get away with the loot."

"Her trail was too cold once we figured it all out. No way to track her. We've lost her, and you've lost Scott, so we've about had it."

"What do you mean?" Dave asked.

"Well, with you laid up for at least a few months, there's not going to be much chance of catching up with him."

"A few months?" Dave scoffed. "Give me two days," he said firmly.

Jim watched the pain streak across Dave's face and didn't argue with him, but he knew Dave would be lucky to be able to sit up in bed in two days.

Two days later, Dave rode out of town. Jim Bates, the doctor, and Charley Thompson watched him ride slowly and painfully out of Abilene.

Thompson shook his head.

Dr. Eric pulled thoughtfully on his white beard. "I'd say he'll be lucky to get one or two miles without all his wounds opening up. He'll bleed to death before tomorrow."

Jim looked after Dave. "Revenge can do amazing things to keep a man alive. The man he's after killed many people Dave cared about. He's got a good deal of rage driving him. He'll make it."

Chapter Fifteen

Dave had never felt such pain before. Scott and his men were six days ahead of him, but two more pressing problems occupied his mind and energy that first day. The first was simply to remain in the saddle, the other to keep his wounds from bleeding excessively. He was afraid to get off Chocolate because he was sure he wouldn't have enough strength to climb back on.

Late in the afternoon, he passed out in the saddle, but Chocolate moved slowly and steadily forward. Finally, after nightfall, Chocolate came to a halt and stood silently on the trail.

A prairie schooner pulled by two oxen and towing two horses rolled up to Dave and Chocolate. A man standing more than six feet eight inches tall removed his floppy, wide-brimmed hat and ran a hand through his short, curly red hair. He laid his long whip up against the wagon and spoke softly to another man, and they quickly climbed down and approached Chocolate.

"What do you think, Doc?"

"He's bleeding badly, Red. Lucky to still be alive, I'd say. Get him into the schooner and let me look at him. He's not going to give us any trouble in his condition."

The redheaded man lifted Dave easily from the saddle and laid him gently in the back of the covered wagon. Doc skillfully re-dressed Dave's wounds, while Red unsaddled Chocolate and tied her to the back of the schooner with the other two horses.

Doc handed Red some papers from Dave's pocket. "He's an Army major. Also working for Wells Fargo. He must've been in a really bad gunfight."

After they were satisfied with their efforts, the schooner moved slowly on toward the Santa Fe Trail.

And so, though Dave didn't know it, he was once again on the trail of the Undertaker and his men.

Chapter Sixteen

Late the next day, Dave slowly forced his eyes open. He studied the buffalo robe covering him with a frown, trying to understand where he was. He smelled something familiar and with some effort turned his head slightly to the right and saw baskets of fresh apples beside him. He looked up and saw dancing shadow on canvas. His eyes closed for a moment, but he forced them back open. He didn't like being out of control. He wanted to sit up but discovered that he didn't even have the strength to move. He cleared his throat and tried to speak, but only a tiny groan emerged.

The schooner bounced when a stranger to Dave jumped in and smiled down at him. "Glad to see that you are awake, Major Kramer. You had us worried."

Dave tried again to speak, but no words came out.

The man nodded. "You want to know where you are, who we are, and what happened, right?"

Dave managed a weak smile and nodded.

"I'm Doc Whitfield. My brother . . ." He yelled, "Hey, Red, stick your head under the canvas and say hello to our patient. He's finally awake."

The canvas lifted, and a grinning face appeared. "Hello, Major Kramer."

"We found you passed out on your horse. I fixed up your wounds, and we have your horse tied to the back of the schooner."

Dave finally managed to whisper, "How do you know who I am?"

"Found your papers in your shirt while I was replacing your

bandages. Impressive credentials. From the number of wounds, you must have been in quite a battle."

"Yeah," Dave said.

"We're heading down to the Santa Fe Trail. After we picked you up and started on our way, your wounds began bleeding again. I realized that it would be better for you if we stopped until you were stronger. Are you going south? If you are, you're welcome to travel with us."

"Yeah, I am heading south." Dave managed a small smile. "And since I don't seem to even have the strength to move, I'd be much obliged if you were to let me travel with you."

"Good. We'll camp here for a few more days and give your wounds time to heal more. Then we'll start again. Riding in this schooner, even with a sack mattress, is not a good way to help you heal."

"Sorry to hold you up."

"Oh, we don't mind. Now, let's see if we can't get some broth down you. Red baked an apple pie that he claims will speed your healing better than his broth, but I'll let you decide."

Dave sniffed the sweet cinnamon smell that filled the inside of the schooner. "Maybe I'll try one bite of the pie for its healing quality, then the broth," he whispered with a smile.

Chapter Seventeen

After a week, Dave could sit up in the prairie schooner. Doc Whitfield managed Dave's wounds as well as any doctor he'd ever seen, yet he told Dave that he wasn't a real physician. Dave could tell that he was healing, but he didn't like how long it would take to get his strength back.

As they traveled, the larger brother, Red, walked beside the oxen. Dave didn't have much experience with oxen, and he was interested in watching how Red worked. He walked beside them and, using a long whip, cracked it occasionally over their heads. He never struck the beasts. As Red told him, "I'd never want to hurt a living thing, but oxen aren't too bright, so they need a little sound to keep them going. Sometimes I yell, but the whip really pops their hooves."

They usually started at dawn and traveled until noon. Then they let the oxen rest and graze until late afternoon, when they started out again. Red explained that oxen didn't handle the summer heat well, and the break ensured that they stayed healthy and strong. During the afternoon breaks, Red would bake either bread or a pie with baskets of apples in the back of the schooner—the smell Dave had first awakened to after they'd picked him up.

Dave found it amazing that a man as large as Red would be such a wonderful cook. The back of the schooner had been outfitted with a chuck box where Red stored all his supplies. Red explained that he had always loved to cook and that his grandmother had taught him how to use a Dutch oven. When he was baking, he was constantly hopping around the fire, turning the Dutch oven every ten to fifteen minutes to make sure his pie was evenly cooked. After a week, Dave felt that eating Red's baked goods was almost as responsible for his getting better as Doc's care.

Doc and Red frequently checked behind them, as though expecting something bad to come storming after them at any minute. Dave never asked, but he figured they were being hunted by someone, or thought they were.

Each evening they stopped, Red would build the fire to reflect its heat back into the schooner. Doc didn't want Dave sleeping on the cold ground and made sure he was tucked under the buffalo hide and kept warm each night. Dave felt a bit like a little boy, with all the fuss being made over him. Still, since he'd been shot, the cold made his muscles and wounds ache, so he was grateful for the warmth under the buffalo pelt.

Red and Doc didn't volunteer any information about where they had come from or where they were going. Dave, on the other hand, needed to talk about Jedd Scott. He didn't realize just how much venom he carried inside him until he started to talk about his return to Quiet Valley.

Dave was surprised to discover that Red was only twenty. His hugeness made him seem far older. He had curly red hair and a curly red beard, but Dave was most impressed by Red's size. Dave figured he had to be nearly seven feet tall, with a broad chest and huge shoulders and arms. When he helped Dave walk around, Dave felt like a child next to him.

Doc was a few years younger than Red and was small and wiry, with piercing dark eyes and straight black hair. He was usually dolefully quiet. Dave was fascinated by Doc's hands—long, thin, and delicate. Dave could easily see them being the hands of a surgeon.

Doc constantly held a large .44 Dragoon Colt. When they rode on the schooner together, Doc would frequently draw from his sitting position and fire at a small rock or berries on a bush.

Dave was aware that Doc could draw and fire much faster than he could—faster and more accurately than anyone he'd ever seen.

The Dragoon was a large, heavy gun, and it took time to reload with the factory-made cloth cartridges. Dave watched Doc practice, day after day, even though he was already an expert at handling the Dragoon. That impressed Dave. Doc carried extra loaded cylinders that he exchanged with amazing speed. Dave recalled seeing some guerrilla fighters using them, but he'd also seen one explode in the hands of a careless man. He didn't think that would happen to Doc.

Dave could chat easily with Red, but with Doc, it was a different matter. It wasn't that Doc was unfriendly; rather, Dave felt that Doc was carrying his own private hell around inside him.

One night, after they'd been on the trail for twelve days, Doc turned to Red and said, "I want him to know. To see what he believes. What do you think?"

Dave realized that Doc wanted to include him in a hidden inner circle yet was anxious about doing so.

Red, however, was clearly comfortable with Dave. "You know I think we should. We haven't been able to think straight since it happened."

Dave listened to the conversation with interest. He had found their behavior strange yet had never probed. Still, he was curious.

Doc gazed into the glowing fire and laced his fingers together over his knees. "Red and I aren't really brothers. I reckon you might have figured that out for yourself. A diphtheria epidemic killed his folks about fifteen years ago. My parents brought him into our house when I was three, so, as far as I'm concerned, he's always been my big brother.

"We're from a little place called Elk Forks in Montana Territory. Our father died two years ago. A rancher next to our place started calling on our mother. Ross Butcher was smooth, but we saw through him. My father's brother, Uncle Herb, was concerned about it, but Momma was lonely and wouldn't listen to any of us.

"A couple of weeks ago, Butcher started pressuring Momma to marry him. Herb visited Butcher and told him to back off. We found Herb a mile from town, shot in the back. We started into town to find the town marshal when two of Butcher's men tried to ambush us."

"Doc shot them both," Red interjected.

"First men you ever killed?" Dave asked.

Doc nodded sadly. "One man I shot told us before he died that three of Butcher's men killed Herb—the Huffman brothers and Frank Richie. But he died before I could get him to sign a confession.

"We rode into town after dark and told Tom Frost, a miner and lumberman and a good friend of the family. Tom was horrified, but he knew that Butcher owned the town marshal, and he felt the marshal wouldn't be any help. He was fearful for us.

"Before we could do anything, Butcher came into town, claiming we'd killed our uncle and two of his men.

"When Tom found out about that, he gave us twenty-seven dollars, and we got out of town. We stopped and told Momma what had happened, and she agreed that we needed to get away until everything settled down. Butcher's got money, and we figured that he'd frame us and have our necks stretched.

"We had this old prairie schooner and the oxen, so we loaded it up as best and as fast as we could. We knew if they came after us on horseback, we could never outrun them, so we hid in a camp of some Indian friends. When we thought it would be safe, we started for Missouri. We didn't imagine that Butcher would send bounty hunters out for us."

Red took over the story. "We were two weeks out of Elk Forks when a couple of bounty hunters showed up. We'd stopped for lunch. With these oxen, we weren't covering ground fast—about fifteen miles a day—but we didn't think there was a rush. With us out of the way, we figured Butcher would be pleased and leave us alone."

"Had the town marshal sent out warrants for you?" Dave asked.

Red and Doc stared at each other. Doc shrugged. "I don't know. Could he have?"

"It's possible," Dave said thoughtfully. "But probably not. Go on. The bounty hunters showed up and . . ."

"They rode up to our camp. Doc saw them coming and had a hunch they were looking for us. He told me to stay by the fire and act normally, just keep cooking. He said if anything happened, hug the ground. They rode in fast, and when they got within a few feet of us, the man in front smiled and said, "Afraid you won't be eating lunch today," and they started to draw their guns. Doc shot them both out of the saddle before they had a chance to blink. Neither one got off a shot."

Doc said, "One man lived for a few hours and told us a bunch."

Red explained. "He told us they were each given a twenty-dollar gold coin to kill us. Then they were to go to the nearest telegraph and send Butcher a message saying, *The lark bunting aren't migrating this year,* so he would know that we were dead. We sent the message instead."

"Smart." Dave said. "Won't those men be missed when they don't go back?"

"The dying man said they were on their way back home to Missouri. That people would assume we'd gotten away, and they'd just continued on home."

Dave sat silently for a moment. "Do you think Butcher told your momma that you're dead?"

"Doesn't much matter," Red said softly. "We can't go back and fight a big outfit like Butcher's."

"Does this Butcher care about your momma?"

Doc shook his head. "No. It's not our mother he wants. It's control of the water in the region. We built a dam ten years ago that gives all the ranches a steady water supply. The man who controls our dam controls all the ranches and farms. Red and I think he wants that."

"Yes." Dave nodded thoughtfully. "Evil men and their dreams of power." He grew quiet, while he thought about what Doc and Red had told him. Finally he asked, "You feel sure this Tom Frost is all right?"

Red grinned at Dave. "We were hoping Momma would be inclined toward Tom. He's not flashy like Butcher, but he cares. Tom arranged for Doc to enter New York Homeopathic Medical College in the fall."

"It's a new program," Doc explained with an enthusiasm that Dave hadn't seen from him until now. "It believes in a more natural approach to medicine and the human body. They don't believe in bleeding patients to heal them. They are interested in using the best methods to cure the sick and injured. William Cullen Bryant, the great poet, started the medical school."

"A poet started a medical school?" Dave asked in surprise.

"Well, not exactly," Doc clarified. "He championed getting the college started. He really got them going. Wasn't that wonderful of him? The school doesn't believe in using leeches or strong drugs, and they want their doctors to understand anatomy and physiology and be more sensitive to the needs of the patient." Doc stopped abruptly and grinned sheepishly at Dave. "I'm really excited about it."

"I can see that," Dave said, smiling. "And now what are you going to do?"

"We don't know." Red looked at Doc. "Going to medical school has been Doc's dream ever since I can remember. But it takes money, and what we've got left won't make it. There's transportation to New York, then tuition is a hundred dollars year, plus the cost for books and supplies and living expenses. It takes three years to complete. We decided there wasn't any use continuing to Missouri to get a train to New York. We couldn't even afford tickets. We thought perhaps we'd join a wagon train, head for California, and dig for gold."

Puzzled, Dave asked, "Dig for gold?"

"Once we get enough gold, then we can go to New York and get Doc his schooling," Red explained.

Doc looked at Dave. "But one day Red and I will return to Elk Forks, and the sword will be in the other hand."

Dave knew that he meant what he said. "It hasn't been a great summer for any of us, huh? Gents, I'm not going to suggest anything to you tonight. I need some time to ponder what you've told me. For now, I want you to let me think on your problem. I survived a civil war, and I can damn well figure out some way to help you two survive your own private war. All right?"

Red and Doc glanced at each other and nodded. Doc smiled at Dave. "Thanks."

Chapter Eighteen

The trail to Wagon Bed Springs was dangerous. Red had taken the road from the Santa Fe Trail to the Cimarron Cutoff, and after they crossed the Arkansas River, they knew they had to travel a long way to get to the next water at Wagon Bed Springs.

Doc checked his map. "It's about ninety miles before we reach water. That should take us six days. I'm glad we filled the barrel. This next stretch looks really barren."

Doc had rubbed charcoal on their faces to protect them from the glare of the sun, and it did help. They all looked like owls, and Dave smiled every time he looked at one of them, although he knew he must look equally funny. Dave had ridden Chocolate across the Arkansas, but now he rode in the wagon. He still tired easily, but every day for the past week he'd been riding Chocolate a few hours longer. He stared out at the flat, desolate prairie with no landmarks and said, "They say that Jedediah Smith got killed by Comanche near the springs looking for water."

"Thanks," Red mumbled as he walked beside the oxen and occasionally cracked his whip with a sharp snap above their heads. "You couldn't tell me something cheerful in this heat, could you?"

Dave laughed. "What's the matter, Red? Don't you like the scenery or the heat?"

Red glanced around him. "Everything's the same wherever you look. It's the flattest prairie I've ever been on. No landmarks, no way to know what's east or west. If this trail wasn't here, I'd be lucky to know up from down." He shook his head. "And if I were an Indian, I wouldn't be walking in this heat. They're probably watching us right now and saying, 'Look at those foolish white men traveling in this heat.' "

Doc said, "No, Red, they're probably saying, 'Look at that big white man with the gorgeous head of red hair and bright red beard. Won't that look good on my belt? ' "

"Doc!" Red exclaimed, but Dave and Doc began laughing so hard at his indignant expression that even Red started chuckling. But he did pull his wide-brimmed hat even lower on his head.

Late in the day, off on the horizon, a buggy came into view, seeming to simply rise up out of the flat prairie in front of them. Red turned and asked Dave if he saw it too. They'd all seen their share of mirages today, so Red wasn't sure. In the distance, the buggy stood as silent and cold as a skeleton. Doc, on his horse, rode up to the schooner as Dave stood up. Dave pulled his hat lower on his head to shield his eyes from the blistering sun. High above the buggy, he saw turkey vultures circling. "Looks like the real thing, but let's move up slowly. Doc, keep an eye behind us." They'd seen signs that morning of a small band of Indians, so they were all wary of a trap.

Once they were closer, they saw that the buggy was off the trail and leaning precariously. A dead mule lay twisted on the ground in front of it, the body covered with flies, and a putrid stench drifted over the area. A number of vultures jumped away with grunts and hisses when they rode up, but they did not fly away. They stared at the humans with irritation at having their meal interrupted.

Dave climbed down stiffly from the schooner. His limp almost gone, he bent down on his good knee and studied the dead mule. He waved a hand in front of his face as a multitude of flies buzzed around. He explained to Doc and Red what he figured had happened. "Something must have spooked it, maybe a rattler. It jerked off the trail, hit that slope, stepped in that hole"—he pointed to a spot underneath the buggy—"and broke its leg when it fell. The other mule must have fallen on top of it."

"Where's the other mule?" Red asked.

Dave reached over and lifted some of the harness. "Look at this. See? It's been cut away. I suspect the second mule went crazy, so the owners had to cut the harness to free it." Dave studied the ground around the dead mule. "It looks like the other mule took off once it was free. That's odd."

"Could it have been Indians?" Doc asked.

"I don't see any signs of that. Very strange."

"This is certainly no place to be on foot." Red looked into the buggy and asked, "I wonder what happened to the owners."

Doc said, "No towns nearby. In this country it would be hard to walk anywhere, but perhaps they tried to make it to the Arkansas. That's closer now than Wagon Bed Springs. But we would have passed them."

Dave said, "I agree. This didn't happen that long ago. We should have passed them. If they tried to make it to the springs, that would be a long and dangerous walk."

Doc agreed. "But they could make the Arkansas, couldn't they?"

"Yeah, if they didn't run into any Indians, they could. But trying to keep your bearings in this country . . . hmm, I don't know." He shook his head. "If I had to walk that far in this heat, I'd look like that dead mule."

Doc grinned at Dave's joke.

Dave studied the ground, trying to make sense out of the mule and footprints. "It looks like it might be just one person, and he went . . ." Dave pointed toward the north, when suddenly something moved in the tall grass in the direction he was pointing. He reached to draw his Adams, but Doc had already drawn his Dragoon.

A woman raised herself from the grass where she had hidden herself and laughed hysterically at them, waving her hands up and down. They stared in bewilderment at the bizarre sight. The turkey vultures took flight.

Red asked, "Has she gone mad?"

Dave stared at the emaciated woman. She looked familiar. He shook his head in disbelief. "Sally?" he called. "Sally Blackfoot?"

The woman stopped laughing and cocked her ear in his direction. She started laughing again, but Dave knew he was right.

Red looked at Dave and asked, "Is this the woman who betrayed her father?"

Dave nodded slowly, still not believing what his eyes told him was true. She stood only twenty feet from them, a skeleton-thin creature, laughing and jumping up and down.

The desert had done horrible things to her. Her hair flowed wildly around her shoulders, uncombed and unkempt. Her clothes were torn and covered with grime and filth. Her face and arms were badly sunburned, covered with scratches and bruises. She started to run away but collapsed and fell into a small, frail heap.

Doc ran up to her and rolled her gently over. He motioned to Red. "You'd better take her to the schooner. She's in a bad way."

While Doc tried to doctor Sally, Red and Dave scrutinized the buggy. Red asked Dave, "Why did she stay here? You said she was part Indian; she could have made it to the river—maybe travel at night when it's cooler."

"I agree. Not only that, but look—there's still food in this buggy. She shouldn't have ended up like this."

"I thought you told us she was heading for Mexico. This buggy was heading back toward Kansas."

Dave nodded. "That's what Jim Bates of Wells Fargo thought." He reached over the side of the buggy and tugged on one end of a chest strapped behind the seat. His eyebrows shot up. "Red, lift this chest down for me, will you please?"

"Which one?" Red asked.

Dave tugged on a second chest and slowly nodded. "Both of them."

Red started to lift the first chest but paused when he realized its weight. "Wow, what's in this thing? It's heavy."

"As heavy as gold," Dave said.

Red got a better hold and with some effort plopped it down onto the ground. Then he lifted down the second chest.

Dave opened the lid of the first one. He saw clothes and personal items in it. He threw aside the clothes, took his bowie knife, and pried up a false bottom.

Red stared at the contents and whistled loudly. "How much is there?"

"I reckon about twenty-five thousand dollars." Dave picked up a twenty-dollar Liberty gold coin from the chest and tried to judge its weight. "I figure each of these must weigh about an ounce. What do you figure the chest weighed—seventy or eighty pounds?"

Red nodded.

"I would guess there are about twelve hundred coins here. That should figure out to be about seventy-five pounds of gold. You can count it if you'd like."

"No, I believe you."

"Check the other chest. Should be about the same amount in it."

Red opened the other chest to confirm.

"Sally Blackfoot split it up so she could lift it. Lifting a hundred and fifty pounds is a bit much for any one person—even you, Red."

"Well, I would have to grunt some." Red smiled sheepishly.

Dave rolled his eyes at Red's reply. "You see?" he said, turning serious. "That's why she stayed. Greed. She was afraid to walk out for fear someone else would find this." Dave sighed deeply. "Damnation. Her father's life for this?" He stared up the trail. "I think she's heading east because she decided she wanted it all for herself. So much for her great love of Jedd Scott."

"I don't understand," Red said. "Where has she been?"

"Good question. Perhaps near Fort Union? It's close to the Cimarron Cutoff and the Santa Fe Trail." Dave shook his head as he tried to figure out her plan. "She must have traveled from Livermore, over to the foothills, and turned south. Came straight down and picked up the Santa Fe Trail over Raton Pass and then holed up near Fort Union to see if Scott would show up. She might have figured that she'd be safe near the fort or a town nearby."

"What if Scott did show up and found her?"

"She could just say she was having buggy or mule trouble. If she still had the money, he wouldn't be suspicious. If they expected to meet in Mexico, and she knew he was heading east for a while, she knew she had to wait long enough to be sure she didn't run into him when he turned back this way."

Red nodded. "Then, when he didn't show up after six weeks or so, she figured he had turned south, and she could head east and disappear."

Dave thought about that and finally shook his head. "Nah, too risky."

"You mean running into Scott and his men?"

"Yup. Since she didn't know when he would turn south, there was too great a chance she could run into him. Way too iffy. She had to be sure that wouldn't happen." Dave thought for a moment longer. "She knew she had to be far enough south that she wouldn't miss him. That would be Fort Union. He'd have to come either on the Santa Fe Trail or the Cimarron Trail and then stop near Fort Union for supplies. There would be no chance she would miss him. If she could hide out there and wait until he showed up . . ."

"And if he didn't see her . . ." Red added.

"Right, if he didn't know she was there, he'd get his supplies, thinking she was ahead of him, maybe already in Mexico. He wouldn't spend much time near the fort. After what he did at Quiet Valley and Livermore, he knows he has a reputation. There should be notices posted about him offering rewards. He'll head for Mexico, where he'll be safe, thinking he's a rich man. Once she saw him leave, she would head in the opposite direction."

Red nodded. "Not a bad plan. By the time Scott got to Mexico and found out she'd stolen his money, he could never get back fast enough to catch her, even if he dared return. She'd get to a railhead first, and after that . . ."

"No way he'd ever be able to track her," Dave finished Red's thought.

"And since she had all his money, he couldn't afford to chase her back east, even if he wanted to," Red added.

"I wonder how close we are to the truth. Ah, well, we'll probably never know." Dave grinned up at Red, picked up a handful of gold pieces, and let them fall noisily back into the chest.

Red listened to the sound of the gold pieces and shook his head with a laugh. "That's sure a pretty sound!"

Dave said easily, "And if you wanted to take it, I don't have strength enough to stop you. I mean, any man who can lift a hundred and fifty pounds and only grunt a little . . ."

Red laughed long and loud. "Ha! You didn't even have enough strength to lift them down from the buggy."

"All right, rub it in."

Red laid a huge hand gently on Dave's shoulder and said with a smile, "But taking it from you would be about as safe as taking a baby grizzly from the mother bear." He laughed again. "And not enough strength? You with four bullet holes in you, still chasing Jedd Scott. I'm big, but I'm no dummy. There're not many men I'd step aside for, but you're one I would. No thanks." Red paused, then added, "Anyway, money comes and goes, but friendship is forever."

Dave smiled up at Red. "Well, my small buffalo, you may end up with both."

"How's that?"

Dave grinned easily and said, "Later. I'll explain later."

Red stared at Dave curiously but didn't question him. Red heaved up the two chests and placed them securely in their schooner.

Red had the oxen go on down the trail, downwind and away from the smell and flies of the dead mule. That evening, Doc told Dave he was being moved out to the ground so Sally Blackfoot could rest in the schooner. "She has some illness, but I'm not sure what. This sun and heat have cooked her good."

"Will she make it?" Red asked.

Doc shrugged. "She's bad off."

They took turns sitting by the fire, watching for Indians throughout the night, but all they heard was a pack of wolves that came to feast on the mule.

In the morning, when Doc checked the schooner, Sally was gone. They spent the morning looking for her, but she had vanished. Red kept saying, "I can't believe none of us heard her leave." Dave studied the sky to see if any of the high-soaring turkey vultures might give him a lead, but they were still dining on the dead mule.

"The sun and sickness disoriented her mind," Doc explained. "I think she was near blind as well."

Dave gazed out over the treeless plains and said softly, "She'll die out there, and I don't really care." He sighed. "I don't like what I've become. I used to care about people, and now all I do is carry this brooding hate inside me." He turned to Red and Doc and added sternly, "Don't you ever let hate do to you what it's done to me. You understand? I know how you feel about what happened to you back home, but don't let it destroy you."

They nodded solemnly. They hadn't seen this dark side of Dave, and it obviously made an impression on them.

Dave turned and stared out over the plains for a long time without speaking. When he finally turned back to them, he had a smile on his face. "We need to talk, gents."

They sat on the shady side of the schooner. Dave took a small notebook from his pocket and wrote busily for a few moments. When he finished, he explained, "We are sitting on fifty thousand dollars, in the middle of Indian Territory, between the Arkansas River and Wagon Bed Springs. You two have a serious problem."

"We have a problem?" Doc asked, puzzled.

"Absolutely. You have to be in St. Joseph, Missouri, to catch the train to New York, and you're going in the wrong direction."

"Dave, I don't have the money to go to medical school."

"Exactly. That's why you two have a problem. You have to get to St. Joseph, Missouri, turn in the gold, collect the reward, tell Jim Bates to send fifteen hundred dollars of it to my father, Robert Kramer, and then you are to use the rest for medical school."

Red stared at Dave, not quite certain what he was hearing. "How much is the reward?"

"Jim Bates said he'd give ten percent of what we get back. I'm guessing that most of the gold is there, but if it's not, just divide what there is of the reward money by thirds."

Doc whispered, "That'd be thirty-five hundred dollars for us."

Red frowned and added, "Wait a minute, thirty-five for us and fifteen for you isn't fair. You should be getting more."

"Close enough," Dave said with a shrug. "Don't go counting pennies." He grinned at Red. "Sure glad *I* don't have to fool with protecting all that money."

"But that's your reward," Red said.

"No, Red, that's *our* reward." Dave leaned back against the wagon wheel and grinned. "See? I told you I could handle your problem."

"But what about you?" Doc asked, pointing toward his wounds.

"Hey, come on, you're one fine doctor. I'm not completely healed, but I'm getting around all right. I'm slow, but I'm steady. I'll be fine."

"You're going to just let us take all that money and then go wobbling off into the sunset?" Red said seriously.

" 'Wobbling'? What's this 'wobbling' stuff, you young buffalo?"

Doc glanced at Red. He had a huge grin on his face. Doc threw up his hands. "I don't know what to say."

"Good, then I don't have to listen to any foolishness. Here's two notes to Jim Bates. Give him this one first, and show him the gold. Give him the second note after he's counted the coins. He'll help you once you get to St. Joseph. He works for Wells Fargo, and he'll be a good contact for you.

"You should find him staying at the John Patee House. That's a big four-story hotel on the corner of Twelfth Street and Pennsylvania. You won't have any trouble finding it. But remember"— Dave looked seriously at them—"if you don't get the gold back, no medical school. Understand?"

They nodded and tried unsuccessfully to look solemn, but they couldn't stop grinning.

"I'm going to ride on into Fort Union and see if Sally Blackfoot did stop there. I want to see if our theory was close. I'll also check and see if they've seen or heard anything about Scott. If he did stop by for supplies, he probably did it quickly and quietly. Not much chance of getting his trail, but we'll see. I'll take enough water with me to make it to Wagon Bed Springs. You shouldn't have any trouble making it back to the Arkansas River."

They agreed.

"I don't need to tell you how dangerous your role is. This is more money than most people will see in ten lifetimes. Not a word to anyone about what you're carrying. Once you get to Missouri, I don't want you to tell anyone except Jim Bates, and only when you're face-to-face with him. If he's not around, you find out where he is and send word that Dave Kramer said it was urgent that you talk to him immediately. He'll come fast. He's a good man."

"Are you going to wire him that we're coming?"

"Too dangerous. If word leaks out that you have that money, no telling who might come after you. We can't chance it. You two, with this old schooner and oxen, are not going to arouse any suspicion. If anyone should ask why you're heading east, just tell them you changed your mind about California and are going back home. Happens often enough, so no one will think a thing of it."

"When do we leave?" Red asked.

"Right now. It's midday, so we both can make some distance before nightfall."

"Right now?" Doc said, surprised. "That quick?"

"That quick. Sometimes that's how life is," Dave said.

Doc nodded. "That's how it's been this summer." He sighed softly and said, "We're going to miss you."

"Me too, Doc. But we'll see each other again. I feel it in my holey body."

Doc tried to smile at Dave's joke but could only manage a small nod.

Red saddled Chocolate and made sure Dave had plenty of supplies. Doc gave Dave's wounds one more look and urged him sternly to keep the wounds clean and change the bandages often. Finally Doc gave Dave a gentle hug.

Dave said playfully when Red tried to do likewise, "No hugs, or I'll end up in the back of the schooner again."

"We owe you. We owe you more than I can say, and someday we'll repay you."

"You can repay me by making sure Doc becomes a real doc. Nobody likes a quack."

Doc snorted and managed a smile, though he had tears in his eyes.

Dave took Red's huge hand in his and softly but firmly shook it. "You take care, my young buffalo."

Red's voice choked as he said, "We've got your address. We'll send a wire to your father once we get the money to your friend. We'll write you in Quiet Valley and tell you where we are. You've got to promise to let us know when you get Scott."

Dave nodded. He pulled himself slowly into the saddle and tipped his hat. He would miss them.

He turned south. He heard the crack of Red's whip as the oxen turned the prairie schooner around to go back to the Arkansas River.

No one looked back.

Chapter Nineteen

By midafternoon of the third day after he'd left Doc and Red Whitfield, Dave arrived at Wagon Bed Springs. He'd just stepped down from Chocolate when he heard the sound of horses and wagons. He reached for his Henry, then stopped when he saw the flag off in the distance. It was a detachment of Army cavalry coming to the springs, escorting settlers in six wagons.

Some moments later, the lieutenant leading the group stopped his column directly in front of Dave. The lieutenant had bright red hair, blue eyes, reddish-brown eyebrows, and a fair, slightly sunburned face. He leaned over and without a smile, said, "I'm not sure that's worth going through to avoid a sunburn."

At first Dave wasn't sure what he was saying, until he realized that the lieutenant was referring to the charcoal Doc had rubbed on his face days earlier. He grinned, reached up, and ran a hand over his beard and face. "From the looks of your sunburn, you should have tried it."

The lieutenant gently patted his own cheek. "The curse of having fair skin. You must be Major Kramer."

"That's correct," Dave said in surprise. "How did you know that?"

"Ran into two men in an old prairie schooner heading toward the Arkansas. They told me about you, and one of them gave me this." He reached into his pocket and pulled out a charcoal stick. "I guess I should have tried it."

"How are they doing?"

"Moving slow but steady to the Arkansas River when we met up with them. They seemed eager to get home to Missouri. I see many on their way to California who turn back. This journey is not for everyone." He suddenly remembered and saluted smartly. "Sorry, Major."

Dave laughed. "Now, Lieutenant, first, I'm not in uniform, and, second, I'm not feeling very military at the moment. How about a handshake?"

"Those Whitfield men said I'd like you." He dismounted and held out his hand. "I'm Lieutenant Jerry Bailey, of the First California Volunteer Cavalry."

With his thick neck and broad, muscular shoulders, the lieutenant seemed taller than his five-foot-seven height, but his legs were shorter than average. He had large, strong hands and a friendly smile, and his handshake was firm. "It be all right if I just call you Jerry?" Dave asked.

"Except in front of the commanding officer, if you don't mind."

"He by-the-book?"

" 'Fraid so. I'm hoping you're not, sir."

"Nope, and Dave will do fine." Dave paused, then added, "Except in front of the commanding officer."

Jerry laughed. "Agreed. We plan to stay here tonight. Will you camp and eat with us, and we can all ride into Fort Union together?"

"Sure, but I'm surprised," Dave said.

"About what?" Jerry asked.

"You didn't say I could camp with you only if I washed up first."

Jerry snickered. "You won't catch me giving orders to a major, even if he does have a mighty dirty face. Of course, with my sunburn, who am I to pick on you?" Then his eyes twinkled. "Except maybe just that one time when we first met."

At dinner that night, Jerry filled Dave in on Fort Union. Dave hadn't realized how large the garrison was. Jerry explained, "In the summer we were up to three hundred fifty troops, but not when I left. Now we have about two hundred men. Maybe twenty or so under arrest, ten or more sick, and one hundred and fifty on duty around the Territory."

"What do they have you doing?"

"This," Jerry said with a wave of his hand toward the wagon

train. "We escort the settlers from Fort Union to Fort Larned and then back again."

"How often?"

"The garrison has escorts twice a month, on the first and the fifteenth. It takes about thirty to thirty-five days to get there, so there's a bunch of us out in the field all the time. We get a little break at Fort Larned and then bring the next train back to Fort Union. General Carleton is serious about these escorts and watching out for Indians. Each man in my troop is carrying one hundred and twenty rounds of ammunition, and the general has made it painfully clear that a man who doesn't have his weapon with him every moment will face serious charges."

"Is this tough duty?"

"Nah, not bad at all. There's all sorts of construction going on at the fort, with perhaps four hundred or more civilians working on building. I'd much rather be out in the field than overseeing a work crew."

"Been in many Indian fights?"

"Just a few. More skirmishes than anything. No direct attacks." Jerry paused. "I saw a reward poster for Jedd Scott, the man you're after."

"Not surprised."

"They're offering two hundred and fifty dollars for him. That's a sizable amount. You after the money?"

Dave stared hard at Jerry. "After I get him, there won't be enough left for anyone to identify. This hunt is not about money."

"Yup, that's what your friends said, but I wanted to hear it from you. Colonel Willis, our commanding officer, knew Major Bates. He'll be interested in talking with you."

Chapter Twenty

Fort Union was in the foothills of the northern Territory of New Mexico, west of the Turkey Mountains and east of the Sangre de Cristos. Lush grassland spread out in every direction. The fort was a sprawling supply center with many new buildings under construction, large corrals filled with horses and mules, and lots of wind. Like everyone else, Dave rode into the fort with a mask over his face against the dust and sand blowing from the north. The wind roared dry and fierce, making it almost impossible to see.

Dave was relieved to get indoors and out of the wind. Lieutenant Jerry Barley took Dave to Bill Moore, the camp sutler, so he could purchase fresh clothes. Jim Bates had provided him with pants and a shirt in Abilene after he'd been shot, to replace what he'd bought in Livermore, but he didn't have any spare. Jerry explained that if he had silver with him, he would get a better price. Dave remembered the pouch Jim had given him when he left Quiet Valley. He hadn't touched any of it, so when he poured the coins from the pouch into his palm, he met immediate laughter from Jerry.

"Major, you're a rich man. You'd better not flash that about. Cash is scarce in these parts." Jerry stopped and looked quizzically at Dave. "You look like you didn't have any idea how much was in that pouch."

"I didn't." Dave explained to Jerry how he'd gotten the money.

"You tell your friend that you know a poor lieutenant at Fort Union who would be happy to take all the extra pouches he'd like to share."

Jeff R. Spalsbury

Dave cleaned up in Jerry's quarters. They were to meet with Colonel Willis at dinner call at noon sharp.

Colonel Willis, dressed in full uniform, stood near the dining table when Jerry and Dave entered the room. Both men saluted. There were six other officers in the room, and the colonel quickly introduced each of them.

Once the colonel sat, the other officers seated themselves around the large table. Dave was on the colonel's left, Jerry beside him. Colonel Willis said, "I was stationed with Major Bates and his wife for eighteen months at Fort Leavenworth. They were good friends. I'd like you to tell me what happened at Fort Livermore."

Dave explained how Major Bates had ridden out to protect the ammunition wagons and had been killed in an ambush by Jedd Scott and his men. He left out the part about the fort being left without guards. He then explained that the troops had come to Quiet Valley, a fight had occurred, and many had been killed. When he was done, the table was quiet.

Finally Colonel Willis said, "You didn't mention the gunfight at Abilene."

"A careless moment, sir."

"As I understand it, Major, mere days after that encounter, you, with four bullet wounds, were back on your horse, tracking this man Scott again."

Dave nodded quickly, feeling his face start to flush.

Colonel Willis removed some sheets of paper from a pouch and handed them to Dave. "Review these, and tell me if they are accurate."

Dave took the papers, and a small smile formed on his face as he scanned them. Jerry, sitting beside Dave, was able to see some of the material and inadvertently mumbled, "Damn!"

Dave's eyes flicked to Jerry, but he didn't say anything. "Yes, sir, they are correct," he said, as he handed the papers back to the colonel. "May I ask how you got them? That information about me is usually classified."

For the first time, Colonel Willis smiled. "I wanted to be sure the best man possible was on the trail of this monstrous killer— the murderer of my friend Major Bates. Our general was kind enough to intercede and obtain your records for me. When I reviewed your war record, I knew the Army had chosen wisely."

"Well, sir, I don't know about the 'wisely' part, but I can assure you that I have very personal reasons for this search."

"And is it your plan to capture this man and return him for trial?"

Dave stared down at his plate for some moments. He carefully chose his words. "Since it is likely that Scott has traveled to Mexico, where we have no jurisdiction, it may be difficult to—"

"Major Kramer," Colonel Willis interrupted. "You don't seem like a man who normally dawdles with an answer."

"You are correct, sir. I'm sorry." Dave frowned and then said firmly, "No, sir, I do not plan to return with Scott once I find him."

Colonel Willis picked up his napkin and placed it in his lap. "You realize, Major, that such action is not sanctioned by the U.S. government."

"Yes, sir, I do."

Colonel Willis nodded. "Which means that there is nothing I can do to help you in your task."

Dave nodded, disappointed but showing no expression.

The colonel helped himself to meat from a platter and passed the platter to Dave.

There was not a sound from anyone at the table.

"However," the colonel said, "it would not be considered 'helping' you if I were to tell you that no one of Scott's description has entered or left this fort in the last two months."

Dave handed the platter to Jerry and turned his full attention back to the colonel.

"Also, I wouldn't consider it 'helping' you if I were to direct you to a small village, Loma Parda, some seven miles from here, where I suspect such a scoundrel might stop for supplies."

Dave contained a smile and nodded seriously. "Thank you, sir. I wouldn't consider that 'helping' me at all."

"Good. It's important to have a clear understanding regarding such matters." Colonel Willis leaned toward Jerry. "Lieutenant Bailey, I believe you are familiar with this village?"

"Barely, sir."

"Barely, Lieutenant?" Colonel Willis said with a serious look on his face.

"Yes, uh, yes, sir," Jerry stammered.

"Hmm. If you say so, Lieutenant. After dinner, I will issue you a two-day pass. I want you to escort Major Kramer to Loma Parda and see what assistance you can offer him."

"I will do my best, sir."

"Lieutenant Bailey, you know what I think of Loma Parda?"

"Yes, sir. You believe it is a vile, immoral, and festering community filled with thieves, prostitutes, and cutthroats who will resort to any action to rob our soldiers of their money and self-respect."

"Very good, Lieutenant." The colonel stared sternly at Jerry. "Certainly not a place for a lieutenant under my command to visit or spend time in."

Jerry gulped. "That is correct, sir."

"But if a certain lieutenant were to know of some of these thieves and cutthroats, he might be able to help Major Kramer get the information he desires."

Jerry sat back in his chair, his face ashen. "Yes, sir. If such a lieutenant did know of some of them, he would certainly know where to take the major."

"Then I suggest, Lieutenant, that that is what needs to be done."

Chapter Twenty-one

Jerry Bailey mumbled to himself as he and Dave rode to Loma Parda. Dave grinned and asked, "What's the matter, Lieutenant? Did the colonel's intel shock you?"

"Don't you be starting that 'lieutenant' stuff with me. I didn't think he had any idea that I was visiting Loma Parda. I bet he knows that I've taken my men there too."

"It wouldn't surprise me," Dave said. "A good commanding officer would know, and it strikes me that not much gets past Colonel Willis."

"That was the longest dinner of my life."

"Yes, as I recall, you never said another word the whole meal. How long have you been going to Loma Parda?"

"More than six months. What should I do?"

"Don't ask me. Remember, my action is not sanctioned by the U.S. government," Dave said with a chuckle.

"Right! And there's no way the colonel can help you, but, oh, by the way, Scott has never visited the fort, and why don't you take that lieutenant who's been sneaking off three or four times a week and have him introduce you to some of the thieves and cutthroats he knows in Loma Parda." Jerry pulled off his gloves and slapped his knee with them. "You know, I do my job well, and my men respect me." He took off his hat and scratched his curly red hair. "And I do speak Spanish."

"Perhaps the colonel thinks you might prove useful if there's any problem between the town and the garrison."

"Well, there's always problems between Loma Parda and the

garrison." Jerry grew quiet for a moment. "What were you and the colonel talking about by yourselves after dinner?"

"He just told me to get that bastard Scott, but that was off the record."

"Nothing about me?"

"Oh, he did mention something about your having no desertions or trouble from your men. That you were fearless in battle and took every assignment without complaint. That your men respect you and your superior officers hold you in high esteem," Dave said.

"Well, that's not bad, huh?" He smiled and straightened up in the saddle.

"Yup, but he also said your moral habits were of serious concern."

"What? Did he really say that?"

"No, I just made that last one up." Dave grinned at Jerry. "Look, it doesn't seem that the colonel is going to throw you into the stockade anytime soon, so enjoy your two-day pass."

"Thanks, I will. It may well be my last." Jerry grinned at Dave. "At least I can ride in with a real war hero."

"Don't you be starting that. What were you doing looking over my shoulder anyway?"

"It was hard not to see. Impressive stuff."

"Not for the men I left behind."

Jerry grimaced. "I'm sorry. I never saw that sort of action."

"I hope you never do. There's no heroics in watching your friends die." Dave asked, "Who are you going to take me to?"

"Loma Parda is not that nasty a place. It has dancing, music, and some gambling. Where else can the men go for some entertainment in this dreary, treeless plain?"

Dave grinned at Jerry. "Quit trying to justify your actions. I'm not the colonel."

Jerry sighed in agreement. "I wish you were."

"Who will we go to see?" Dave asked again.

"There's only one person in Loma Parda who would have the information you need, and that's the alcalde."

"The alcalde? I remember that word, but I can't recall what it means."

"He's the boss of Loma Parda. He'd be like a mayor or a judge in our cities."

"That's it, mayor. And does the alcalde like Lieutenant Bailey?"

"I play cards with him every time I go into town."

"You gamble with the alcalde?"

"I lose every time I play with him."

"You lose?" Dave said in surprise. "You don't look like a card player who would lose."

"Hey, it's not easy to lose all the time."

"So why do you?"

"When I play with the alcalde, I never have to buy a drink. And after we play for a while, the alcalde always gets hungry, and we have to stop and eat. His wife is the best cook in the New Mexico Territory. You tasted the food at the fort, and that was for the colonel. Can you imagine what *I* get to eat? Horrible. So I lose a few coins in an evening. I couldn't even buy two drinks for that. The alcalde makes sure my men are treated fairly. Everyone wins."

"Don't you think this alcalde might be on to your shenanigans?"

Jerry smiled. "I think he is, but we both enjoy playing cards and discussing whatever's going on. For drinks and food, it's a good trade."

It took less than an hour to ride to Loma Parda. They passed several small farms. Loma Parda was similar to many towns Dave had seen near military forts. Dave noticed two saloons, a general store, a mill, and even a church. Jerry rode up to an adobe house, where two men came quickly from inside and took their horses.

"Nice service," Dave said.

Jerry went through the house to an open courtyard. The alcalde sat by a fire pit roasting a fat red pepper on a stick. He was a handsome, well-dressed man, thin but muscular, with short, curly black hair graying slightly at the temples. While he greeted them with an smile, his eyes looked suspicious of Dave.

Jerry introduced Dave and then said to Dave, "This is the alcalde, Señor Ruben de la Rosa."

Dave repeated the name slowly. "Ruben de la Rosa." A slight smile formed on his lips.

A woman brought white Mexican wine to them. They sat across from the fire pit while the alcalde continued roasting his pepper.

Jerry explained in Spanish what Dave needed. He asked about Sally Blackfoot, but the alcalde shook his head. Then Jerry asked about Scott, and again the alcalde shook his head and spoke to Jerry in Spanish.

Jerry turned to Dave. "I'm sorry. If anyone would know if these people had come through, it would be the alcalde. He says that he does not know of either of them."

Dave nodded and studied the alcalde closely. He leaned forward. "Alcalde, let me tell you a story. . . ."

Jerry started to translate, but Dave waved him to be still.

"But, Dave, he doesn't understand English."

Dave nodded but continued. "When I was a young boy living high in the Rocky Mountains, I helped a Mexican man, a teacher, who had the misfortune of getting trapped in his wagon while traveling in winter. He did not speak English, but my father spoke a little Spanish and invited him to stay with us until the snows melted and it would be safe for him to continue. The teacher felt uncomfortable living with us for nothing, so my father suggested that he teach me Spanish in return. The day that he was to leave, I went to him to say good-bye and thank him, and he said to me in perfect English, 'It has been a great joy staying with you and teaching you Spanish.' Well, I was amazed that he could speak such perfect English, and I asked him why he'd never told me this before. And he said, 'Because my big brother told me that . . .'"

Dave paused, smiled at the alcalde, and spread his open hands toward the man to finish his statement.

Jerry glanced from Dave to Ruben de la Rosa, totally confused.

The alcalde removed a cigar from a box and, using a twig from the fire, carefully lit the tip, inhaled deeply, and blew three perfect smoke rings. There was total silence in the courtyard. Then he smiled at Dave and said in English, "Because if the Anglos don't know you understand English, you can quickly learn if they are your friends or your enemy."

Jerry gasped, and Ruben and Dave laughed in unison.

"All this time, Alcalde, you could speak English!" Jerry exclaimed. "This has not been a good day for me."

Ruben laughed again. "It's all right, Lieutenant. You have showed many times over that you are a friend. Even if you didn't always leave a donation at my card games, my wife says that no one eats her cooking with more joy than you do."

"Amazing!" Jerry pointed a finger at Dave. "And that means you speak Spanish."

Dave shrugged. "The alcalde spoke wisely. His brother, Rafael de la Rosa, taught me well."

Jerry took a large gulp of wine. "I hope you realize that in one day you've turned my life completely upside down."

Dave laughed at Jerry and asked Ruben, "How is my wonderful teacher?"

"Rafael lives now in California, in San Jose. He has many daughters. I remind him that a few boys are in order, but he delights in his girls." Ruben laughed. "He spoke often of you. How you and your family saved his life and the pleasure of living with you. I did not make the connection when the lieutenant first introduced us. My apology."

"I am honored to meet you. Rafael held you in high regard, but I never thought I'd meet you in person."

"This calls for a party." Ruben clapped his hands. Three servants hurried into the courtyard.

"Food?" Jerry said hopefully.

Ruben laughed. "Yes, food, drink, music, and dancing. The man who helped save my brother's life must be treated as an honored guest."

Ruben stood and placed a hand on Dave's shoulder. "We will talk later about these people you search for. If I were to tell you all I know now, you would not stay."

"After listening to Jerry rave about how wonderfully your wife cooks, I would be very foolish to even consider going without enjoying her food."

Ruben laughed at Dave. "And what else did my brother teach you?"

"If I were ever to meet your sister, I'm not to use any of the words she teaches me, because they will not be polite words. And if anyone from your family tells me that the food is not that hot, don't believe them. But if I should be so crazy as to taste it and find my mouth on fire, I must never drink water; only milk will put out the flame."

Ruben laughed again. "Yes, he taught you well."

Late that night, Ruben and Dave sat again in front of the fire pit, each with a glass of white wine. Dave smoked his battered pipe, and Ruben smoked a cigar. "The lieutenant has told me why you search for this man. I am sorry."

"He has killed many innocent people."

"The woman, Sally Blackfoot, *was* here. An odd woman. She brought me a twenty-dollar gold piece and asked me to hide her for two months. I found a place where she could place her buggy out of sight, and her mules were kept in a corral where they blended in with all the others. I offered her a place to stay, but she insisted on sleeping under the buggy.

"Then she changed what she was wearing to look like an old Mexican woman. She wore a baggy dress and a sombrero that was far too large for her; it hid her face. She would sit behind a stone wall, hidden from riders but where she could watch the road.

"And that's what she did every day for hours. In the evenings, she would go to each saloon and stop and look inside to see who was there."

Dave nodded. "We thought that's what she might be doing. It's good to know that our hunch was correct. She was waiting for Scott."

"Yes, the bad man you call Scott. He, too, was here, twelve days ago. One day after he left, the woman left. I'm sorry I did not tell you right away, but I had to determine whether you were friend or foe."

"I understand. Did Scott kill anyone here in Loma Parda?"

"Yes, but it was not as you might think. In the saloon, his men were all drinking heavily. One of them got too drunk. He started talking about how The Ghost was going to come to get them all."

"The Ghost?" Dave asked in confusion.

Ruben leaned back in his chair and drew on his cigar, clearly enjoying the moment. "The Ghost that was hunting them. You!"

"Me?"

"As far as they knew, no one in the saloon spoke English, so I heard much about how you have been hunting them. At first they thought it was the son of a man they had killed for guns, but then they realized it was someone else. They don't know who you are or why you are hunting them, but they claimed that you never stop. They called you The Ghost."

Dave's face showed his surprise. "What happened then?" Dave asked.

"This Scott became upset with his man and took out his gun and shot him dead."

"Shot his own man?" Dave exclaimed in surprise.

Ruben shook his head, still not believing it himself. "Immediately, another man started yelling at Scott, saying they were not supposed to get into trouble here, and now look what you've done. They drew their guns. I had eight or nine men in the saloon at the time and all of them lifted their shotguns. This Scott man realized they were greatly outnumbered. My bartender motioned for them to leave. And that's what they did."

"And now they are down one more man," Dave said softly.

"Yes, but they are still dangerous men—and more will likely join them. That type always draws evil ones."

Dave nodded. "Any idea where they went?"

"The Territory of New Mexico is large. There are many trails where one can cross over into Mexico, if they chose to do so. They may remain in the mountains close to the border, where they can hide, or in small villages they can take over." Ruben puffed his cigar, and Dave waited, somehow knowing that Ruben had more to say.

"I heard that they were almost out of money. This Scott is not a man who will work for money, so wherever there are people he can rob and kill, that's where he will go. The dead will guide you."

Dave nodded. "Thank you for your hospitality, Alcalde. You have honored me with your food, drink, and music. You have touched my heart. I must leave in the morning." Dave paused. "But not until after breakfast."

Ruben smiled. "My brother taught you well. I will write you a letter of introduction. It may prove useful as you travel throughout the Territory."

The next morning, Dave rode south. Scott's trail had gone cold, but Dave's wounds were healing, and his meeting with Ruben de la Rosa had rejuvenated him. The search, he realized, could be a very long one. Scott would go into Mexico, expecting to find Sally Blackfoot waiting for him. Once he realized that she'd stolen the gold, he'd return to New Mexico to rob and kill some more. Ruben was correct. The dead would guide him.

Chapter Twenty-two

A cold, torrential rain poured from low-hanging black clouds when Red and Doc Whitfield stopped their wagon across the street from the John Patee House in St. Joseph, Missouri. People hurried by with their umbrellas flapping in the wind. Red and Doc felt out of place with their rough and dirty clothes. Red looked up at the hotel and said, "That's the biggest, fanciest building I've ever seen."

Doc stepped down from the wagon and nodded. Rain ran off the brim of his hat.

"What are we going to do?" Red asked, as he stepped down on the other side.

"Just what Dave told us to. We're going in there to find Jim Bates."

"I'll watch the wagon."

"You sure you don't want to go," Doc asked, "and I'll watch the wagon?"

"Nah." Red stepped back. "You'll be better at that than I would."

They stared at the building. "This sure is a big town," Red said. They heard the sound of a locomotive nearby. "I reckon it's the biggest town we've ever been in."

Doc took a deep breath. "All right. I'm going." But he didn't move.

Red asked, "Do you want me to give you a little shove?"

"I'm working up to it, all right?"

"Hey, I understand. I sure don't want to go in there."

Doc frowned at the building. A couple hurried by in the rain and stared at him. Doc glared back. "I wish people wouldn't stare at us."

"Yeah, that doesn't seem real friendly, does it?"

"Okay, here I go." Doc took one hesitant step and stopped.

"You're getting closer," Red said.

"Thanks."

Doc took two deep breaths and finally walked across the street and into the John Patee House. His pants and shirt were soaked by the time he stepped inside.

The desk clerk glanced up at him nonchalantly. Since the hotel was the headquarters for the Pony Express back in 1860, and many Pony Express riders had stayed there, he was used to seeing rough, trail-weary men come in.

Doc said hesitantly, "I'm looking for Jim Bates of Wells Fargo."

"Mr. Bates, right. I just saw him." The clerk leaned over the counter and pointed toward a sitting area in the lobby by the front window. "He's over there, just past the fireplace."

Doc looked unsure. The clerk added, "With the tweed jacket and gray mustache, talking with those three other men."

"Right." Doc nodded his thanks and approached the group. One man glanced up at him and snickered. "That's a big gun. You know how to use it, or do you just wear it to scare people?" The man stood and opened his suit coat to reveal a shiny new Colt around his waist. Everyone in the group grew quiet.

Doc was stunned by the threat. For a moment he thought of turning around and leaving the hotel, but then he got angry. He took two steps back, wiped his hand dry on the seat of his pants, spread his legs, and let his arm drop to his gun side. "Fine. Make your move." His voice was low and ominous even as water dripped from his hat.

The man with the Colt glanced at his friends. "Hey, I was just kidding."

"I'm not," Doc said calmly. "First you insult me, and then you threaten me? I'm going to show you that I know how to use my big gun—by killing you."

The man jerked back against the chair. He waved his hand

back and forth, trying to signify *no*. Sweat broke out on his forehead and ran down his face.

Jim Bates stood and stepped between the two men and said firmly, "Max, apologize to this man, then sit down. And if you say one more word, you're fired."

Max nodded rapidly. "Sorry," he whispered. "I'm terribly sorry." He sat quickly and looked down at his hands, too fearful even to glance up at Doc.

Jim turned to Doc. "I'm sorry about that. He was rude and thoughtless."

Doc nodded and added, "And stupid."

Bates agreed. "Yes, and stupid." He took a deep breath and asked, "Was there someone here you wanted to talk to?"

Doc continued to glare at Max, and Jim became concerned. "He's from Philadelphia and never carried a gun in his life till he arrived here. It's a new experience. He was stupid to confront you, but he did apologize."

Doc nodded slowly. "I've traveled a long distance to speak to Mr. Bates." He glared at Max. "I wasn't expecting to meet something like him in a place like this. Perhaps in a saloon, but not here."

"Again, I'm sorry. I think you just taught him a valuable lesson about the West."

Doc sighed. "A lesson, yes. How to come dangerously close to dying." Doc twisted his neck from side to side to relax his tension. He took two deep breaths, then asked, "Are you Jim Bates?"

"I am."

"My name's Doc Whitfield. Dave Kramer sent me to you."

Jim's demeanor changed instantly. With a wave of his hand, he motioned for a man to give his chair to Doc. "How is Dave? Where is he? Is he all right?"

"He's fine." Doc shook his head at the offered chair, reached inside his vest, and handed Jim the first note Dave had written.

Jim quickly unfolded and read the note. "Dave wants you to show me something."

"It's out in the wagon." Doc glanced at the three men. "Can they be trusted?"

"They work for me, for Wells Fargo. I vouch for them."

Doc frowned at Max but turned and led Jim Bates out of the hotel. The other three men followed.

Red stood in the rain beside the prairie schooner. The rain dribbled off the brim of his hat. A flatbed wagon drawn by four horses narrowly missed the schooner, splashing his pant legs and boots, before parking behind him. Two rough-looking men stepped down and glared at Red but then looked at the hotel and started talking quietly to each other. Red stomped his boots to shake off the water. He thought of saying something to them about their wagon driving but decided to ignore them when he saw Doc and the four men hurrying from the hotel. The rain had turned into a light drizzle.

Doc quickly introduced Red to Jim Bates, and they climbed under the canvas cover, out of the drizzle. The two chests were strapped down. The other three men climbed up and looked into the wagon from the front bench, where there was a little shelter from the rain.

Jim, Red, and Doc stood hunched over the chests. Doc dried his hands on an old piece of cloth and said, "Dave said I was to show this to you but only face-to-face." He lifted the first chest lid and removed the hidden bottom board, exposing the gold coins.

Jim reached down and picked up a handful of coins. "He found Sally Blackfoot?"

Doc nodded.

Jim turned and showed the coins to his three men.

"Is this the gold that Jedd Scott stole?" one of the men asked.

Jim nodded and asked Doc, "How much did you recover?"

"We've never counted it, but Dave thought most of it was here."

Jim said, "Well, first we need to—"

"Get your hands in the air," a gruff voice demanded from behind them. They turned to the back of the wagon, where the two men from the other wagon stood holding their revolvers pointed directly at them.

Slowly they lifted their arms into the air.

"Kind of you to save us the trouble of robbing the hotel.

You"—he motioned at Red—"can just lift that chest over to our—" He stopped when he realized that Doc had not lifted his hands. He pointed his gun at Doc. "Are you hard of hear—"

The man never finished his sentence. Doc drew, and three shots reverberated inside the covered wagon.

Doc's first shot struck the bandit just above his left eye and flung him over backward in a wild somersault. The second thief glanced at his friend in surprise just as Doc's next shot hit him in the chest. His revolver spun out into the street as he was lifted from the force of the shot before he crashed into a puddle, spraying mud and water in all directions. Neither man had fired a shot.

Jim Bates stared at Doc Whitfield and then at the two dead men lying in the street, puddles of water slowly turning red from their blood. Women screamed, and he could hear people running toward them.

"My God," Jim whispered, "I've never seen anything like that in my life." He turned and glanced at Max. Max was glassy-eyed and pale. His mouth was wide open, but he made no sound. The other two men stared at Doc in amazement.

Doc slowly slid his Dragoon back into his holster. Red took a deep breath and said to Jim, "Trying to take that gold from Doc was personal. Doc promised Dave Kramer he'd get it back to you safely. He takes his promises seriously."

"I just saw that." Jim sat down on the second chest and breathed deeply. "Give me a moment, all right?"

Shortly after the shooting, the police came to haul away the bodies of the robbers. The gold was safely moved to a bank under armed guard. Doc gave Jim Bates Dave's second note, and after reading it, Jim said they needed to stay the night at the hotel. He arranged for them to have a room on the same floor as his. He told them to go clean up and buy some new clothes while he handled everything. He also made arrangements to sell their wagon, the oxen, and their two horses.

Late that day, Jim sat with Doc and Red at a private restaurant. They could finally talk at length without being interrupted. Doc and Red both wore new wool suits, and both had haircuts and were clean-shaven.

Jim nodded approvingly at their appearance. "You look like fine young businessmen." He handed a ledger sheet to Red and explained, "This is the count of the gold coins and what your share is. I got a fair price for your wagon, oxen, and horses, and that's included too."

Red nodded as he read the ledger page. "So they only spent two hundred dollars." He handed the sheet to Doc.

Jim explained, "You will each receive a third of the reward money. I've already made arrangements to send Dave's father his share."

Doc took a pencil and quickly added. "That's three thousand dollars for us." He grinned at Red.

"Actually, Doc," Jim said, "it's more. You need to add the sale of your wagon and stock. Then there was a hundred-dollar reward for each of the two wanted men who tried to rob us. So you need to add two hundred dollars more."

"It doesn't seem right to take money for killing men," Doc said.

"No, perhaps not," Jim agreed. "But those men were wanted for killing innocent people, so that money is a way for those dead people to say thank you."

"I guess so." Doc frowned down at his hands.

"Doc," Jim asked, "did you ever read the two notes that Dave wrote to me?"

"No, sir. Those were private notes for you."

Jim smiled. "Well, that doesn't surprise me about you. In the first note, Dave told me to go with you and look at something he'd sent for me. That, of course, was the two chests with the gold in them. In the other note, he told me about your dream to become a doctor. He asked me to help you. Considering that you traveled all that way with fifty thousand dollars in gold coin that you could have just as easily taken off with, I figure that's the least I can do."

"Well, sir, that's not quite true," Red said.

"Oh? How's that?"

"Would you want Dave Kramer after you?"

Jim laughed loudly. "That's a valid point, Red. But even if there wasn't a Dave Kramer, I still think you'd have brought the money to me."

Doc nodded. "Yes, sir, that's true. We were raised to be honest."

"I thought so."

Red added, "And Dave Kramer is our friend, and we promised him."

"Yes, promises are not to be taken lightly. Well, I made a promise to Dave as well, and that was that any way I could help, I would. I've telegraphed some friends in New York, and all the arrangements have been made for you to attend your medical school." He reached into the breast pocket of his suit coat and removed two tickets. "These are your train tickets to New York, compliments of Wells Fargo. A close friend of mine, Larry Swartz, will meet you at the train when you get in and help you with whatever you need."

"Sir, we don't know how to thank you," Doc said, his face glowing with a wide smile.

"You already did when you saved Dave Kramer that night on the trail. As you know, Dave is after the man who killed my brother. My company is delighted to get their gold back, but since what happened to my brother, Major Bates, this has never been only about the gold for me."

"We understand," Red said. "Dave explained it to us. We are sorry for your loss."

"Thank you, Red. That's kind of you." He looked away from them for a moment and took a deep breath. When he turned back, he had composed himself. He asked, "Red, what about you? Your brother is off to medical school, but what do you plan to do in New York?"

Red nodded thoughtfully and glanced at Doc. "I was telling Doc this afternoon that I want to make sure he's settled in all right, and I want to visit the school he'll be going to, but I don't want to stay. I'm not comfortable in big cities, and I understand that St. Joseph is tiny compared to New York."

"New York is much bigger," Jim agreed.

"Well, I've decided I'm going to take a ship to California and head for the gold fields."

"So, you're going to dig for gold?" Jim said. "Even with all your reward money?"

"Nope. I'm going to open a bakery," Red said with a huge smile on his face.

"A bakery?" Jim exclaimed in surprise. "Why a bakery?"

"Because Dave told me that when I bake my bread and pies, those miners will give me all their gold for them. And that would be more fun for me than digging all day and, if Dave is correct, more rewarding."

Jim sat back in his chair and nodded. "Dave mentioned in his second note that I should try one of your pies. I wasn't sure what he meant, but now it makes sense. And that's why you didn't want me to sell your two Dutch ovens. I think Dave is correct—those miners will pay anything for home cooking. And here I was, about to offer you a job with Wells Fargo. I need someone to take Max's place."

"What happened to him?" Doc asked.

"He resigned after he saw you shoot the two thieves. He decided that he wasn't cut out to be a Wells Fargo detective after all." Jim started laughing. "He told me that he didn't even see you draw. He'll probably tell his grandchildren years from now about the time he challenged the fastest gun in the West."

Doc shook his head. "That's not a title I ever want to have."

"And I notice, Doc, that you aren't wearing your gun. Good."

"I thought about what you told me, sir. I have to tell you, I keep reaching down for it, but as you said, it's a different world where I'm heading."

"You have no idea how different, Doc. You'll get used to not wearing a gun faster than you think."

Doc absently reached down to his side. "I suppose so."

Jim looked at them thoughtfully. "Are you both going to be all right?"

Doc's eyes suddenly filled with tears. "Red and I have been together since I was three. It's going to be hard for me, not having him by my side."

"I know it's going to be a rough adjustment for you both," Jim said, "and you should expect to be homesick for a little while.

That's normal. However, after a time you will be so busy with your lives that the separation won't hurt so much. The railroads are pushing hard to get a track to California. Before you know it, you'll be able to jump on a train and travel back and forth and visit each other. You have enough money, so if you spend it prudently, that shouldn't be a problem."

He paused and handed each a small envelope. "This has my address and how you can contact me. If you ever have any trouble, you just telegraph me." He frowned and then added, "And I want to know how you are both doing. I expect you to drop me a letter sometime. Will you do that for me?"

"Yes, sir."

"Wells Fargo's headquarters are in San Francisco, so Red, once you have an address, send it to me. I've got to stop and eat one of those pies Dave says I should try. Doc, I know where you'll be. Although I don't get to New York too often, when I do, I'll come by and see how you are." Jim stood and held out his hand. "Safe journey. This certainly has been one of the most extraordinary days I've ever had. Godspeed, gentlemen."

Chapter Twenty-three

Dave's first stop was in Las Vegas. In the central plaza, he used Ruben de la Rosa's letter to get the local alcalde's trust quickly. He asked if Jedd Scott had been through there and was told that three men robbed a man bringing supplies into the town days ago. One of them fit Scott's description. "Did they kill the man?" Dave asked.

The alcalde shook his head. "No, but they beat him with a pistol. He was badly hurt. They were gone before we could track them, but it looked as though they were heading south."

Dave shook his head sadly. "I'm sorry."

As he rode out of Las Vegas, he remembered what Ruben had told him—you will follow the dead. Ruben should have included the wounded as well. Scott's men *must* be low on ammunition if they weren't shooting to kill.

In Santa Fe, he stopped in at the town marshal's office and showed his credentials and the reward poster for Jedd Scott. There had been no robberies or shootings recently, but three men had eaten at a cantina outside of town and left without paying their bill. The description matched Scott. Dave continued south.

Many days passed as Dave traveled south to the border. In some towns he heard of robberies that might have been done by Scott, but mostly he thought that Scott was hurrying to the border to get to his stolen gold coins. That was the only thing that made Dave smile—imagining what Scott would do once he realized that he'd been robbed by Sally Blackfoot.

Near the border, a month after he'd left Loma Parda, he rode into a small, dusty town. He immediately sensed something wasn't right as he headed slowly up the main street.

He rode directly to the livery stable and stepped down with difficulty. He still felt the stiffness of his healed wounds, and he was bone weary from his long journey. He slung his saddlebag over one shoulder and pulled the Henry from its scabbard. No one was in the stable. He glanced across the street at the saloon. The middle of the afternoon was normally too early for a saloon to be doing much business, yet even from across the street, he could hear the sounds of loud, angry men arguing inside.

A man staggered out of the tavern and stumbled over to where Dave was standing. He spit tobacco juice at Dave's feet and growled, "What the hell you want?"

Dave studied him up and down, and a slight smile formed on his face. He shifted the Henry to his left hand, and his right hand drifted silently down to the Adams. He stepped back slightly and spread his feet more comfortably apart.

The liveryman suddenly realized Dave was setting up to draw on him. "Hey, I don't have no gun."

Dave spoke so softly, the drunken liveryman had to lean forward to hear. "Then I reckon you'd better get one, or take care of my horse. If you get a gun, I'll kill you, so I reckon you'd better just take care of my horse."

The liveryman's eyes opened wide. He'd tried a whiskey bluff and gotten a real challenge in return. He nodded and started saying, "Yes, sir, yes, sir, yes, sir," over and over. He quickly led Chocolate into a stall.

It didn't take Dave long to learn what was happening in the town. He ate dinner at an old, run-down boardinghouse, and the talk around the community table was all about the killer in jail.

"He should be hanged right now."

"That damn sheriff, protecting a murderer."

"Let's do it today."

Dave didn't like the sound of it. After dinner, he walked around the town and felt the tension building.

When the sun vanished in the west, the town finally exploded.

Men streamed out into the street—angry, violent, and drunk. They came cursing and chanting, "Hang him! Hang him! Hang him!"

Dave looked on with horror and fascination, as if watching bloodthirsty wolves ready to satisfy their hunger with human flesh.

The mob stormed up to the jail, and there it met its first test. The sheriff stepped out. He held a shotgun cradled loosely in his arm. He was a tall, older man, with grayish white hair that blew about his head while he stood quietly facing the challenge.

Dave decided the sheriff didn't have a prayer.

If the sheriff was afraid, he didn't show it. He spoke to the crowd in a loud, clear voice, telling them to go home.

Dave shook his head. He didn't want to get involved in this, but the mob, like Scott, seemed cruel and heartless. He checked the load in his Henry.

One final surge of the mob shoved the sheriff back against the jailhouse wall. Two men held the sheriff, while the leader of the crowd grabbed his shotgun. The leader yelled to someone inside the jailhouse to release the prisoner or they'd hang the sheriff instead.

When nothing happened, the man yelled to the crowd to hang the sheriff. They yelled their approval.

Dave's anger curdled. He climbed onto the bed of a wagon across the street from the jail and, taking careful aim, fired off five shots that lifted the hat off the mob's leader and sprayed adobe chips around the two men holding the sheriff. They quickly dropped the sheriff's arms and ran back into the crowd.

In the time it took for the mob to turn around, Dave loaded five more shells into the Henry.

The mob was now facing him. He fired at the feet of the men directly in front of him, and when they jumped aside, he fired again and again until he had cleared a path straight through to the leader. The man stood with his mouth open, in direct sight of the rifleman.

Dave's rapid shots and his skill had already unnerved the crowd.

Dave casually reloaded and with a sarcastic smile fired another shot that crashed into the wall above the mob leader's head.

Adobe chips splashed down on the man's face, and he dropped the shotgun and threw up his arms.

The sheriff picked up the shotgun and immediately took control. "Let's go home, folks. The party's over. The judge will get to town soon enough, and we can do the hanging legally, the way it should be done."

The mob didn't want to go, but it didn't want to stay either. In unison, Dave and the sheriff fired their weapons into the air. That was all the convincing the crowd needed. In five minutes, the only people on the street were Dave and the sheriff.

The sheriff sighed at the sight of the empty street. "Damn it to hell, that's as close to hanging as I want to get. Thanks," he said when Dave walked up to him.

The sheriff motioned for him to go into the jail. Dave was surprised to find that the only help the sheriff had to guard the prisoner was his wife, a tall, slender, pretty woman with long auburn hair and a quick smile.

The sheriff sat wearily at his desk, and that's when Dave noticed how exhausted the man looked. He had a four-day growth of beard and dark streaks under his bloodshot blue eyes. He was a handsome man, with a well-tanned face, thick hair, and bushy eyebrows. His wife handed him a cup of coffee and asked Dave if he would like one. Dave nodded. When he tasted the coffee, he realized it had been fortified with a shot of whiskey.

"Young man, I've forgotten my manners. I'm Sheriff McMakin. This is my wife, Donna." He started to rise, but his wife held him down with a look. He smiled tenderly at her and gave Dave a shrug.

"I'm Dave Kramer. I—"

"Well, Jim was right," Sheriff McMakin interrupted.

"Jim?" Dave questioned.

"Jim Bates. He's an old, old friend. I just received a letter from him about you. Came on the stage, just a few days ago."

Dave shook his head in wonder. Bates really got around.

"That was some fancy shooting out there. Lifting Leo's hat off was amazing," the sheriff declared with a shake of his head.

"Well, to be honest, Sheriff—"

Sheriff McMakin interrupted Dave again. "My friends call me Mac."

"Okay, Mac. That shot was a bit low. I didn't mean for that to happen."

Mac started laughing. "By golly, that's funny." He chuckled for a few moments and then said seriously to Dave, "I have to tell you that you may be sorry you helped stop that mob. That's one of Jedd Scott's men in back."

Dave's face grew hard. "They kill again?"

"Yes." He sighed. "A good family man. We went as far as the border, but they were too fast for us. We shot the horse out from under this one. Apparently, he knew he was going to die alone, 'cause he's been plenty talkative. Told me plenty about you. They call you The Ghost."

"I almost was in Abilene."

"Well, I'm mighty glad they missed. Jim Bates holds you in high regard."

Dave shifted his feet uncomfortably. "Looks like you could use a little help," he said, trying to change the subject.

Donna's look of hope told him all he needed to know.

"Why don't you go on home and get some rest? Don't worry about the prisoner."

The sheriff said, "I don't feel right about that."

Dave smiled at Mac. "Scott's the one I want. Your prisoner will be here in the morning, in the same condition he is now."

"I don't—"

"That's fine," Donna interrupted. "Mac hasn't had a good night's rest for days. I'll bring you back some fine homemade pie, bread, beans, and rice and the best coffee you've ever tasted."

Dave laughed and said, "This isn't too bad, right here," as he motioned to the coffee with the whiskey in it.

Mac slowly and wearily pulled himself out of the chair and smiled his thanks at Dave. "I'll be back in a few hours. Just a few hours, and I'll be as good as new."

At noon the next day, the sheriff came sheepishly into the jail, carrying a basket with lunch for them.

Dave laughed at him and said, "It's a good thing your wife cooks better than you keep time."

Mac held up his hands in mock surrender.

During the next several days, while they waited for the judge to arrive, Dave and Mac became friends.

The town quieted back down, and with Dave Kramer there, no one seemed eager to face "the young gunfighter," as they called him.

At the beginning of the second week, the judge finally came. The trial took twenty minutes and the hanging ten. That was justice Dave could respect.

After the trial, Dave started making forays into the small towns near the Mexican border, using Mac and Donna's home as a base. On three occasions he helped the sheriff deal with some rowdy locals, but mostly the town remained quiet.

Leo Nieman, a drunk who ran the hotel, was the only man Dave didn't like. Dave remembered him as the mob's leader, but Mac seemed more than able to handle him now. The more time he spent with the sheriff and learned about him from the townspeople, the more he admired the strength, honesty, and fairness of the man.

One day, after the stage had been through, Mac came to him with a letter. "It looks as though your man Scott has shown up in El Paso." He handed Dave the letter. "I just got this from a lawman friend down there, and from the description, it's him."

Dave read the letter and frowned. "I always thought he was farther west. Never figured on El Paso. I'll take the morning stage and check it out." He grinned at Mac. "You get stuck with Chocolate's stall duty."

"I don't remember anything about that in my contract when I became sheriff here."

"See how lucky you are?"

Chapter Twenty-four

El Paso turned out to be another futile trip. Scott and his remaining men had been through, robbing and killing, but his trail was long cold. The ride back on the stage was bumpy, hot, and dusty. Dave thought about the past year. He'd seen a five-year war end and a personal war start. Friends had died, and he was no closer to finding Jedd Scott than he was when he left Quiet Valley. He was growing weary of the search.

Suddenly the stage halted. Dave glanced outside. They were in the middle of the desert. No reason for them to be stopping.

A rider with a handgun and a mask rode up to the window and motioned for Dave to put his hands up. Dave glanced out the window on the other side of the stagecoach and saw more masked riders. One was demanding that the safe box be thrown down by the shotgun guard. The masked rider watching Dave glanced up at the driver. That was all the time Dave needed to pull his Adams. He shot the man in the chest. In the same instant, he leaped out of the coach and slid under it, as the other riders opened fire into the coach where he'd been. Dave fired from under the coach and killed another robber, as the shotgun guard blasted the nearest outlaw with both barrels of a sawed-off shotgun. The driver whipped the horses, and the coach leaped forward. Dave grabbed on to the undercarriage as his feet dragged and bounced on the trail.

At the top of the next ridge, the driver pulled the coach to a halt after he saw that the bandits weren't chasing them. The guard leaped down and opened the door of the coach, expecting to find his passenger dead. Instead, Dave awkwardly crawled out from under the coach, spitting dust. He frowned at his mangled boots. Both heels were gone. He was coated with dust and grime from the ride.

The guard scratched his scruffy beard and grinned at Dave. "That was some shooting back there. Sorry about your boots. I thought we'd be taking you to boot hill, but I guess we just need to take you to a store so you can buy some new ones."

Dave sat down on the ground, and the guard pulled the remains of his boots off, as Dave kept spitting dust and brushing pebbles and sand from his clothes.

"Are your feet all right?" the guard asked. He examined Dave's bruised heels.

Dave limped to the coach, reached inside, grabbed his canteen, took a quick swig, and then poured water onto his feet. "My heels feel like they've been fried."

The driver pointed back up the trail. A lone rider sat watching them with a single-tube spyglass. Farther off in the distance were two other riders. Dave stared down the trail. The rider was out of rifle range, but even at that distance Dave could make out his black outfit and skinny frame. He recognized Jedd Scott. He quickly reached inside the coach and pulled out his Henry. Bracing himself against the coach door, he fired off one shot. The distance was too great and he knew it, but the bullet still created a puff of dust in front of Scott's horse as the report echoed over the hills. Scott spun his horse and raced away.

"Damn," the shotgun guard exclaimed, "that was some shot! You almost hit him. You know that robber?"

"Been chasing him for months."

"He must have known you, 'cause once you shot at him, he took off like he'd seen a ghost."

Dave smiled grimly. "He did see one. He thought he'd killed me in Abilene. He must have seen me under the coach and wanted to know if I was his ghost or not."

"You got his attention."

"It's not his attention I want. It's his hide."

When Dave got back to the sheriff's office, he told Mac about the attempted robbery. Mac rubbed his chin thoughtfully. "You'd best be careful. This man knows you will never stop. He knows that he has to kill you before you kill him."

Dave leaned back in a chair and propped his tender feet up on a second chair. "He has to find me first, Mac."

"Yes, but you're easier to find than he is. Damn it to hell, Dave, he'll try to bushwhack you or get someone else to do it for him."

"That has occurred to me as well," Dave replied seriously. "But I'll be ready."

"Be that," Mac said, his bushy eyebrows creased in worry.

Chapter Twenty-five

The hunt for Scott continued, but Dave became more cautious. Mac's warning was clear. Who was hunting whom? Each trip he made to a different border town was filled with unknown dangers. Each time he heard of a killing or a robbery, he'd check it out, but for each slow, agonizing search, there was no success. Christmas came, and Dave realized he hadn't seen snow or been home for Christmas in five years.

The desert in the winter might not have the heat of summer, but it had plenty of cold and loneliness. Each trip Dave made into small villages in Mexico was met with frustration. Had Scott simply disappeared into the desert scrubland, never to be found?

He had been out for three weeks this time, and he still had no clues to Scott's whereabouts. Near nightfall of the third day, as he headed back from the border, he was still a long day's journey away from Mac and Donna's home. He was tired and discouraged.

Gunshots immediately brought him to a full state of alertness. He shifted Chocolate toward what he thought was the direction of the shots. Almost immediately, he realized his mistake and shifted direction again. He'd learned that the desert could play strange games with sounds.

He urged Chocolate through dense sagebrush and scrambled out some distance from a small cabin built into the back of a rocky hill. Eight Indians were firing at the cabin. They hadn't seen or heard Dave's noisy exit from the sagebush.

He guided Chocolate back into the shrubs, pulled his Henry, and swung down.

The Indians rushed across the clearing toward the cabin.

Whoever was inside held their fire until the last possible moment. Not until the first Indian was within ten feet of the cabin did
the person fire. That Indian fell dead.

Dave waited for more shots, but none came.

The Indians crowded against the door and tried to break it
down.

Dave decided that whoever was inside was either out of ammunition or dead. He moved to a rock pile for cover and opened
fire.

It caught the Indians by surprise. Before they could dash away
from the cabin, Dave shot three of them. When they ran from the
cabin to their horses, Dave fired twice more. His shots were low,
and a horse crashed to the ground. The rider landed on his back
with a loud snap and didn't move again.

An Indian by the cabin started to throw a knife, but Dave
caught the movement out of the corner of his eye. He spun and
fired the Henry from his hip, slamming the Indian to the ground.

Dave shifted the Henry to his left hand, pulled his Adams,
and walked cautiously to the front of the cabin. He checked the
bodies.

The cabin door opened, but he only spared a glance at the
woman who was standing there.

When he was sure the Indians by the cabin were dead, he went
to the man by the dead horse. He didn't realize his error until the
woman yelled. He spun and fired at point-blank range, but it didn't
stop the Indian. Dave dropped his weapons and grabbed the
man's wrist just in time to prevent a knife from being shoved into
his chest.

The Indian's rush tumbled them both to the ground. Dave's head
knocked against a rock, and he fought to remain awake. Through
his hazy vision, he saw the knife coming slowly but steadily toward
his chest.

Then there was a low whistling sound and a dull thud. The Indian collapsed to the side of him. Dave rolled over onto his hands
and knees, and slowly his vision cleared. The man lay in a puddle
of blood, an ax blade stuck deep in his back.

Dave rose slowly to his feet and felt his head. A knot was

forming where he'd struck the rock. The woman stared at the Indian she'd killed, her face chalky white.

Dave reached down unsteadily and picked up his Henry and Adams. When he looked back, the woman had fallen to the ground. Dave thought she'd fainted, until he saw the blood. He knelt beside her and felt for a pulse. There was none. This woman had given the last breath of her life for him, and he wondered if he deserved it. He felt tired. He'd seen too much death.

Remembering that two Indians had gotten away, he knew he must check the cabin quickly and leave before they returned. He hurried unsteadily inside, his head throbbing. The cabin was dim, and Dave paused to let his eyes adjust to the lack of light.

He saw a man in a corner, facedown on the earthen floor. Dave stepped over a broken bench and lifted a chair off the man's back. He gently turned the man over, grimaced, and allowed the body to roll back.

He stopped in the doorway and glanced at the mantel with its tintype of a man and a woman with a young girl. From the doorway, he could see the body of the woman who'd saved his life. He frowned at her. She reminded Dave of Mrs. Byrne and how she'd begged him to save her baby, hidden under the bed. He winced at the memory of the Byrnes' house on fire. The throbbing pain in his head made it hard to think. There was a child in the picture. Where was that child?

He looked toward the bed. A dust-filled sunbeam shimmered down onto a corner of the mattress, the sun's last streak before dark.

Was that a movement? He blinked. His head was pounding, and his vision was blurry. He looked again.

He hurried over, reached under the bed, and gently slid out a woman of about twenty. A deep, ugly wound along one side of her head had turned her shiny black hair into a reddish mat.

Dave lifted her onto the bed and carefully cleaned and dressed the wound. She remained deathly still. Her face burned with fever. He pumped water from the well and placed a cool, wet cloth on her brow. He took another cloth, wet it, and held it against the back of his own head. It helped the hammering pain inside his skull.

Darkness made it hard for him to get around, but he was too worried about the Indians returning to risk lighting a fire. He dug shallow graves and buried the woman's mother and father. He tried to bring the woman's fever down with cold cloths, but they weren't dropping her fever. Heat still boiled inside her body.

She needed a doctor. He knew that he couldn't leave her behind to ride for help.

He found an old wagon but no horses. The Indians' horses had run off, and there were none in the corral. Chocolate would have to pull the wagon. He knew how much Chocolate hated doing that.

He moved the wagon up to the cabin door. The desert night had turned cold. He made one last search of the cabin and found an old family Bible, the tintype from the mantel, and some old letters. If she lived, she would at least have some record of her family. He didn't see anything else of value in the house.

Chocolate twisted her head around and looked at the wagon with what Dave perceived as real disgust. "Sorry, old girl, this is an emergency," Dave whispered, as he urged her forward. She snorted, switched her tail in protest, and then started up the dirt road, pulling the wagon.

Dave's mind jumped to the McMakins. He found it strange how quickly a rapport had developed among them. They'd accepted him almost as a son, and he had to admit, he liked the feeling. A mother's concern was a special joy for him, one he hadn't felt since he was ten years old.

Chapter Twenty-six

Dave wearily approached the town at that strange misty time when night and early morning whispered to each other. He'd had no sleep for over thirty hours, but it wasn't the lack of sleep that kept his muscles taut. It was the pitiful, low moans of the injured woman in the wagon. Every bump brought another moan, until he found it hard to breathe, hard to keep his eyes clear of tears. Each moan reminded him of what he'd already lost, of how helpless he sometimes was to help.

He felt the woman's forehead. Her fever had broken during the night, but she remained deathlike. That worried him. Dave placed a new wet cloth on her forehead.

When Chocolate lifted her head and increased her pace, Dave glanced up and saw the McMakins' house on the edge of town. "You know home when you see it, huh, old girl?" Dave whispered to the horse.

When he reached the house, he had Chocolate back the wagon up to the door. He ran up to the door and knocked loudly. He didn't wait for Donna but returned to the wagon and removed the blankets from the woman.

Donna came to the door with her hair hanging loosely over her shoulders. She pulled her robe tightly around her waist and hurried to the wagon. He quickly explained what had happened.

Dave lifted the woman easily into his arms, then carried her into the house and to his bedroom. Donna started to undress her. She told Dave to hurry after Dr. Boyer.

When Dave returned with the doctor, he was beyond exhaustion but tried not to show it. Mac handed him a cup of coffee and followed him out to the stable, where Mac had moved Chocolate. He told Mac about the Indian attack. Mac stopped him and checked the bump on the back of his head. He poked it gently with one finger.

"Hey, watch it. That hurts," Dave scolded.

Mac grinned. "Just a little tender to the touch. Nothing to worry about."

"Thanks, but next time I'll let the doctor check it. Has Donna ever told you that you have a mean streak?"

"Only when it comes to *soreheads*." Mac laughed at his own joke.

Dave let himself fall awkwardly into the hay without spilling his coffee. He grinned up at Mac. "It's a good thing this coffee is better than your jokes." He finished his coffee as he explained to Mac how he'd found the woman. "The memory of Mrs. Byrne kept popping into my head and how helpless I felt that I couldn't save her baby. I kept staring at the picture in the cabin, but my brain wasn't working right. Three people in the picture, but only two people dead. Why'd it take me so long to make the connection? I should have figured out immediately that there might be a third person in the cabin. What if I'd left without checking?"

"But the point is, you didn't leave. Ours is not to judge or sometimes even to understand," Mac said thoughtfully. "Don't be so hard on yourself. You had a nasty blow to your head. It's a wonder you were able to function at all. What's important is that you saved her life."

Dave nodded. When he started to get up to take care of Chocolate, Mac motioned for him to stay, that he'd take care of the horse.

Dave didn't argue. "I think I'll just lie back for a moment." He was asleep as soon as he finished his sentence.

The sheriff chuckled as he pulled off Dave's boots and covered him with a blanket.

When Donna came to the stable, she saw her husband's smiling face, saw Dave, and nodded understandingly. She threw her husband a kiss with her fingertips and went back to the house.

Dave woke just after sundown. He sat up stiffly and pulled off the blanket. He felt the back of his head and was relieved that it was only a little tender to his touch. He was in the middle of stretching when Donna walked into the stable with a lamp.

She smiled warmly at him. "I figured I'd find you up and about. Just when I start cooking, all my menfolk start stretching and acting hungry."

Dave stood and kissed her on the cheek. "Well, you've got to admit, we appreciate a good cook." He walked with her toward the kitchen. "How's the woman?"

"Much better. She's stronger than you thought. Came to late this morning and took some broth. Fell off to sleep again."

"That's good news."

"I might add that she also smells much better than you do right now."

"Does that mean I have to take a bath every three weeks now?"

"David!"

He laughed loudly and gave her a hug. "You sure are a fussy woman."

"Just remember, my food is only served to clean-smelling men."

"That's a terrible rule for a man who smells as earthy as I do."

Donna pointed to the barrel, already filled with warmed water, and handed him a bar of soap.

"Aren't you going to tell me to wash behind my ears?"

Donna shook a finger at him. "A good switch to your behind is what you're going to get." She laughed merrily and returned to the kitchen.

When Dave walked into the kitchen, Mac sniffed loudly and said, "It sure is good to be around you without having to hold my nose." They sat and said grace. Before Mac could continue to pick on Dave, Donna started reminding her husband of some of his trips out and how he smelled when he returned.

The next afternoon, Dave was out cleaning the stable when a shadow crossed his light. Standing in the doorway was a pretty young woman wearing a faded yellow dress and a bandage around her head. Until he saw the bandage, he didn't realize that it was the woman he'd brought in.

He flicked a bead of sweat away from the end of his nose and leaned on the pitchfork. "How are you doing?"

"Better, thanks to you."

He was amazed that she could get up so soon, but if Donna allowed it, it must be all right.

They stood smiling at each other, neither one seeming to know what to say. She took a deep breath, walked in slowly, held out her hand, and said softly, "My name's Elizabeth Donahue."

She had a sweet, gentle voice, and he liked the sound. He quickly wiped his hand off on the back of his pants and took hers. "Hello, uh . . . I'm Dave Kramer." Her hand was small and soft. He held it a bit too long and was embarrassed when he let go. "Did Donna tell you about your family?"

"Yes." A great sadness filled her face, and Dave felt it in his own heart.

"Do you mind," she asked, "if we talk about it some other time?" Her dark, tear-filled eyes rose to his, and he tried to pull his gaze away but found he couldn't.

"Certainly," he whispered.

She turned away from him and went to the window. She looked out at the bleak, silent desert for a long while. Finally, she turned and asked, "May I stay and watch you?" She'd composed herself and smiled more easily when she added, "I might enjoy watching someone else work."

Dave laughed and said, "So. Donna sent a spy out to make sure I don't loaf on the job."

During that afternoon, a tiny flame was lit again in the heart of a man who'd felt sure it had gone out forever.

Chapter Twenty-seven

Dave rode tiredly back toward town. It had been another long hunt with no results. Chocolate quickened her pace without urging. They were within sight of town, and she knew that oats and a rubdown awaited her efforts. Dave expected the streets to be empty this late in the day, but they were too empty, deserted.

Dave pulled on the reins and stared, trying not to think of Quiet Valley. The bank door opened unexpectedly, and Dave spun in the saddle and quickly drew his Adams. Vince McGuire, the bank vice president, came out, turned, and locked the door for the evening.

Dave sighed and slid his Adams back into its holster. He was glad Vince hadn't seen him draw on him. Still, he felt something was wrong. He urged Chocolate toward the McMakins' house on the edge of town.

Before he got there, Todd Anderson, the general store owner, waved him to a stop. "Have you heard?"

"Heard what?" Dave said.

Todd grimaced. "I'm sorry I have to be the one to tell you. I know you and Sheriff McMakin . . ."

"Tell me what?"

"The sheriff was shot about an hour ago."

"God, no!" Dave's voice choked. "Who did it?"

"About a week ago, Leo Nieman brought in some new men to work for him. Everyone knew they were gunmen, and I guess after all the fights Nieman and the sheriff have had, it didn't really surprise anyone.

"Funny thing is, the sheriff told me last evening, he thought the men might be after you. I don't know why. Anyway, about an hour ago, the sheriff was crossing the street, and someone fired at him from a rooftop. A perfect shot."

Dave shook his head. Scott's name kept racing through his brain. It had to be Scott's doing; no one else wanted him. Not that way.

"There's more," Todd said.

"What else could there be?"

"Mrs. McMakin thought that Nieman was responsible for her husband's death. She went busting into the hotel about twenty minutes ago with a shotgun and told him and his cronies to be out of town by eight o'clock tomorrow morning or she'd come gunning for them."

"She couldn't—" Dave gasped, but Todd held up a hand for silence.

"One of the men went for his gun, and Donna shot him dead. The rest were so dumbfounded, she got away. They're talking of hanging her tomorrow morning. The town's frightened. The people are afraid to walk on the street."

"My God! They don't have her, do they?"

"No, I guess they figured there won't be a problem collecting her tomorrow."

"Will anyone in town help?"

Todd looked away from Dave's face.

"I understand. Thanks for telling me."

He rode quickly to the McMakin house, hurried inside, and found the doctor sitting at the table, smiling and drinking a cup of coffee. Dave asked, "Dr. Boyer, what's going on?"

Doctor Boyer shook his head in wonderment. "It's the damnedest thing. That bullet hit the sheriff in the back, circled around his rib cage under his skin, and popped out the front, clean as you please."

"You mean the sheriff's alive?"

"He's hurting, but he's plenty alive."

Dave hurried into the sheriff's bedroom. Mac was asleep in the bed, his chest wrapped in bandages. Donna sat on the edge of the mattress, holding his hand. Elizabeth stood nearby. She saw

Dave and ran to him. Dave clutched her tightly to him and softly stroked her hair.

"What are you going to do?" she whispered.

"I'm not sure. We'll see." Dave went to kiss Donna on the cheek. "How's he doing?"

"Doc gave him something to make him sleep." She looked up at Dave. "I thought he was dead. I'd never have done what I did if I knew he was still alive."

"I know. You just stay with him. He's going to be fine."

Donna nodded.

Elizabeth followed Dave to the kitchen, poured him some coffee, and refilled the doctor's cup.

"Can the sheriff be moved?" Dave asked Dr. Boyer.

"In a few days. That bullet bruised his ribs badly, so he'll be hurting for a month or more every time he takes a breath. He's just lucky to be alive." The doctor added, "He's going to be too weak, though, to be able to help you tomorrow. I'm sorry."

"It's okay. Finding him alive—that's all that's important."

Boyer told Elizabeth, "You call me if he starts a fever."

Elizabeth nodded.

"Dr. Boyer," Dave said, "don't tell anyone that the sheriff's still alive."

Dr. Boyer stopped and nodded thoughtfully. "Yes, I understand. You can count on me."

After the doctor left, Elizabeth started crying softly. Dave gathered her into his arms.

"I know you're going to fight those men tomorrow," she said. "I don't want you to get killed."

Dave said, "This is part of my affair with the murdering Jedd Scott. You know that, don't you?"

"Yes." She looked up at him. "But I've already lost too much."

Dave suggested they sit outside. She sat in the swing and he in an old, squeaky rocking chair. And they talked late into the night.

Chapter Twenty-eight

The stagecoach arrived at 7:45. One person got off, a young blond man carrying a satchel and a Henry rifle. He walked into the stage station and asked the stationmaster in a low, hoarse voice, "Where can I find the sheriff's home?"

The stationmaster was a small, dried-up man with a shiny bald head and a beaked nose. He said, "It's up the road about two blocks, then down the street to the left. If I was you, though, I wouldn't be going up there right now."

"Oh, why's that?" the young man asked.

The stationmaster glanced around suspiciously, fearful some of Nieman's gunfighters might be near. Satisfied they weren't, he leaned close to the young man and said softly, "Since ya's new here, I tell ya, but ya've got to promise not to mention it to anyone, or tell anyone—anyone at all—that I was the one who told ya."

The young man nodded, assuring the stationmaster he would keep still.

The stationmaster told his story with much histrionics and delight. This was the first person he'd had a chance to tell about all the goings-on in town, and he wasn't going to leave out a thing.

The young man listened intently and only stopped him once, and that was to ask the name of the man who was going to fight Nieman's gunmen.

When the stationmaster finished, the young man thanked him and asked if he could leave his satchel. The stationmaster took it and asked, "Ya not going to be staying long?"

"Won't know for a while," the young man replied. He walked away from the stage station with the rifle held loosely in the cradle of his arm.

Chapter Twenty-nine

Dave scowled at the clock above the table and with a tired sigh pushed himself from the chair. He picked up his hat and pulled it low over his forehead. Elizabeth stood staring out the window. She turned her head and gave Dave a quick smile but couldn't hold it and turned away with a slight sob. Donna started to say something, shook her head, and instead checked the load of the shotgun in her arms again.

Dave walked to the door, stopped, and said, "I don't think you need worry, no matter how this all turns out. They're here after me. You stay inside until someone comes and tells you what happened." He looked down the deserted street and said, "Well, see you soon."

Elizabeth turned around and cried, "Dave!"

He stopped. She ran over and hugged him. "Come back. Please come back."

He brushed the tears off her cheeks, then bent and kissed her gently on the forehead. He stared at her face for a long moment, then turned and started slowly down the path.

He knew many hidden eyes were watching him, yet the town had the same abandoned appearance of Quiet Valley. A shiver ran down his back, and he flexed his muscles to relax. Once he reached the main street, he saw three gunmen just leaving the hotel. That meant two others were hiding somewhere, waiting for him. They weren't going to take a chance of his walking away alive this time.

He glanced up and down the storefronts, but they were deserted except for one person leaning back in a chair against the wall by the saddle shop. *Well,* Dave thought, *that's a dumb way to set up an ambush.*

He walked up the center of the street until he was even with the saddle shop. The other three gunmen were still a block away, but Dave wanted to be able to see this back-shooter out of the corner of his eye.

The man in the chair stood slowly and pushed his hat back off his head. Dave glanced at him and immediately did a double take. He tried to wipe the grin off his face. "Damnation!" he said softly.

Ted Jones stood loosely against the post and with his eyes quickly indicated to Dave the position of the other gunmen—one on the roof behind him and one between the gun shop and the land office. Dave nodded slightly to confirm he understood.

The three gunmen came down the street, spread out. The man in the middle called out, "Glad you made it to the show, Kramer. Scott would have been mighty upset if you hadn't shown up."

Dave glanced at Ted. Ted motioned for him to get the two behind him, and he would take the three in front. The post Ted stood beside was large enough to hide his movements. The gunmen knew he was there, but they didn't suspect he was anything more than an eager kid wanting to get a close look at the big showdown.

They didn't have a chance to regret their mistake. Ted stepped out from behind the post, firing his Henry as fast as he could cock it. His first two shots smashed into the gunman doing the talking.

Dave dove to the street as a bullet dug a hole into the ground where he'd been standing. Before the man on the roof fired again, Dave got off two shots. One missed, but the other tore into the man's chest. The man fell off the roof, screaming, until he crashed into an empty wagon parked by the building.

Ted hit the second street gunman with a low shot that rammed him to the street, where he lay twisting and shrieking in anguish.

The third street gunman turned and started to run, when Dave hammered off three shots. The third shot struck the gunman in the back and dropped him to his knees. The man tried to get up, fell on his face, and slowly rolled over onto his back. His body jerked wildly three times and then was still.

The gunman between the two buildings fired two wild shots. Ted spun and blasted him, the force of the shots splaying him against the wall of a shop before he slid to the ground, dead.

The gunman up the street, already shot, tried to aim his gun at Ted. Dave fired his Adams. The gunman smashed back down in the street, dead.

Abruptly, all was still. The screams of dying men were silent. All were dead except Dave and Ted. The smoke from the gunfight hung low to the ground, floating gently over the scattered bodies.

Satisfied that the battle was over, Dave holstered his Adams and grabbed Ted in an emotional bear hug. "Damnation, are you a welcome sight!"

Ted smiled at him and said in a low, gravelly voice, "Needn't yell. I'm not deaf."

Dave's mouth opened and he tried to speak, but only a high-pitched squeak came out. He coughed and tried again. "When the hell did you start talking?"

Ted grinned and explained. "After I got shot in the throat, Dr. Zimms was able to fix my vocal cords some. It's not real pretty, but I sure do love my new voice."

Dave shook his head in happy amazement. "What do you mean, 'not real pretty'? It's beautiful, Ted! Absolutely beautiful!"

"Dave!"

Dave turned as Elizabeth ran up the street and into his arms. Then she leaned back and held him at arm's length. "Are you okay? They didn't hit you anyplace, did they? Who's that? What—"

"Whoa there, girl." Dave laughed. "I'm fine. They didn't get me. Say hi to Ted Jones. I've told you about him. Ted, this is Elizabeth Donahue."

Ted nodded and smiled at her, but Elizabeth gave Ted a hug and kissed him soundly on the cheek. Ted blushed slightly, but Elizabeth laughed and said, "That's for saving Dave. If you hadn't been here, I don't know what would have happened."

Ted nodded and motioned at the crowd of people slowly com-

ing out of the nearby buildings. "You have to wonder if they realize they might have prevented all this."

Dave looked at them. "I'll never understand it."

Ted opened his mouth to speak but was interrupted by the un-
mistakable roar of a double-barrel shotgun.

"Donna!" Elizabeth cried to Dave and Ted's unasked question.
"She's gone after Nieman."

Dave ran toward the hotel with Ted close beside him. Dave
pulled his Adams and shook his head at the empty chambers. Ted
saw his dilemma and flipped his revolver to him. Ted reloaded
his rifle while they ran.

Dave exploded through the hotel door. Even before he could
cry out Donna's name, he saw her flat on the floor, just inside the
door. The shotgun lay behind her against a wall.

Across the room, directly in front of his office door, Nieman
lay in a tangled heap. Donna had fired both barrels of the shotgun into him, and he was a mass of torn, bloody flesh. Dave
guessed that they must have shot each other at the same instant.

Ted bent down to check on Donna. Dave saw Nieman start to
move and was amazed he was still alive. Dave glared down at him
without pity.

Nieman said painfully, "Scott said to take you. Kill The Ghost,
he said. Should've known better."

Dave knelt beside Nieman. "Where is he?"

Nieman smiled bitterly. "Ninety miles southeast, at Noche de
la Cuidad. Go ahead and kill the bastard!"

Dave nodded.

Nieman said in gasping breath, "I just wish . . . I . . . could . . .
get . . . that damn . . ." He never finished.

Dave turned around to help Ted carry Donna's body, but he saw
that they were both gone. He hurried outside. Donna sat on a
bench holding her shoulder and chatting excitedly with Ted. Dave
could barely talk. "You're not dead!"

Ted grinned up at Dave. "Whoever loaded those shotgun
shells must have put in enough powder to kill an elk. I figure the
gun kicked back on her and knocked her out."

Donna looked up at Dave and said, "I'm sorry. I know I shouldn't have done it, but the sheriff is my man."

Dave leaned down. "I thought we'd lost you." He brushed tears from his eyes. "You did fine."

"Well, I don't feel fine. I feel like I broke my shoulder, and I've got a horrible knot on my head." She looked up at Dave and added, "But the McMakin honor is intact."

Ted laughed. "Mrs. McMakin, I just hope you always remember that I'm on your side."

Dave picked Donna up in his arms and carried her over to Dr. Boyer's office. She hadn't broken her shoulder, but as she had said, it sure felt like it.

Later that day, Dave and Ted had a long talk with Mac, Donna, and Elizabeth. Mac and Donna sat beside each other, propped up with pillows on their bed. Dave and his father had written back and forth with an idea, and Ted had brought back the answer he wanted.

Quiet Valley needed a sheriff. People were moving back, and two new mines had opened. Dave's father had organized the necessary paperwork, and Sheriff McMakin was being offered the job.

"I don't know what to say." Mac looked at his wife. "What do you think?"

Donna reached over and took Mac's hand. "I'll go wherever you go—you know that."

Ted said in his gravelly voice, "It's a real pretty place, folks. Beautiful mountains, clear streams, and good people." He glanced at Dave. "Now."

Dave said, "And if you ever need help, you'll have two of the best men in the West to back you up. This place has too much growing up to do. You've done your share here; come back with us. Quiet Valley needs you. I need you." Dave then said seriously, "Of course, it probably would be better if we could get both the McMakins out of bed. Having a sheriff with holes in the front and back of his body and a wife who can't use her arm and just sits around in bed all day . . ." Dave paused and dramatically shook his head. "Well, I don't know."

Elizabeth gasped. "Dave, that's a terrible thing to say after what they've been through. Shame on you."

Donna added, "Good for you, Elizabeth. You tell him. He's getting far too big for his britches, I'd say."

Dave shrugged. "Just making an observation. I can't imagine why you're picking on me. Ted, what do you think?"

"Don't you involve me in this. I'm just trying to keep Donna on my good side," Ted said, struggling to keep from smiling. "She scares me!"

Donna held her shoulder and rocked back and forth on the bed, laughing. "Shame on you, Ted Jones. That's not a nice thing to say either. You are both bad boys."

Mac shook his head. "I can see why you two are friends." He chewed on his lower lip and nodded. "Damn it to hell, all right, by golly, I'll do it. I sure would like to see a white Christmas again, and you two need some serious looking after."

Donna nodded happily, then leaned to give her husband a soft, gentle kiss on the cheek.

"Elizabeth," Dave said, placing his arm tenderly around her waist. "I want you to go with them. You'll stay with my father. There are serious things I need to talk to you about, but not here, not now."

"You and Ted are going after Scott, aren't you?"

"Neither Ted nor I will be free until we've taken care of this thing. Please tell me you understand."

Elizabeth didn't answer.

Ted said, "It's all right. I'll take good care of him. Honest."

Elizabeth hugged Ted. "I know you will. Thank you." She sighed at Dave. "All right. Donna has told me about you two. Be off with you." She took a deep breath. "But come back to us." She reached out and took Dave's hand. "Just know that I have serious things to say to you as well."

Dave and Ted left early the next morning, heading south. Mac, Donna, and Elizabeth left town two days later in a wagon filled with their belongings, heading north toward the Rocky Mountains.

Ted and Dave were quiet as they rode toward the border. They'd seen death come too often and too quickly not to ignore that they might be riding to their own. Yet, for reasons neither of them could verbalize, they knew this would be the last time they would ride after Jedd Scott.

This would be their final turn to hunt the hunter.

Chapter Thirty

Dave and Ted rode cautiously into the small village of Noche de la Cuidad. Outside a cantina, a crowd peered intently through the door.

Dave motioned that they would start there. When they dismounted and pulled their Henrys, a crowd of Mexicans turned and looked at them, then parted quickly to let them through.

They entered a low-ceilinged room packed with silent, fearful men. Dave felt his pulse quicken. Against the back wall, behind a long table covered with empty bottles and dirty plates, sat a thin, ugly man dressed in black with a gunman on either side of him. At the first sight of him, Dave felt a calm come over him he'd almost forgotten—a calm that comes after a long, hard, bitter search.

Jedd Scott and his two gunmen laughed among themselves while a Mexican boy stood facing them. The boy was no gunfighter. His holster was too high, his gun too old and rusty. Dave figured the boy to be eleven or twelve years old.

If the boy felt fear, he didn't show it. His boyish voice was hard when he said in Spanish, "You have disgraced my family. You have disgraced my sister. You are a pig, and I will kill you."

Scott turned to the gunfighter on his left and mockingly said, "My, my, he certainly is a mean one, huh?"

A priest ran into the cantina. "No, no, no, Raul. This is not God's way."

Scott and his two gunfighters were too amused by the priest and the boy to notice Dave and Ted. Ted indicated with his eyes that he was going to move to the bar. That would place them on either side of the room and give them good shooting positions.

The Mexicans grudgingly moved aside as he angled through the crowd to the bar.

When the priest was certain he could not change the mind of the boy, he turned toward Scott and pleaded in English. "Señor, he is but a boy. Surely you will not shoot him. He is from a family of farmers; he has never carried a gun before."

The gunman on the right of Scott stood and yelled at the priest, "Oh, hell, shut up, Godman!"

Scott, also tiring of the game, leaned back in his chair and said, "Kill him."

The priest moved in front of the boy and said bravely, "Then you will have to shoot me first."

For the first time since Dave and Ted entered the cantina, the Mexicans standing inside and outside gasped and murmured their anger. The other gunman stood slowly and deliberately, enjoying their ready-made circus. He said to the priest, "If you want to die, we can oblige you."

A fearful hush fell over the cantina. The priest stood bravely in front of the boy. Ted glanced at Dave. Dave nodded.

Before the killers had their guns drawn, Dave and Ted opened fire with their Henrys. The room exploded with the sounds of the rifles firing and the gunmen's screams as bullets smashed into their bodies.

The firing stopped.

Rifle smoke drifted silently throughout the cantina. No one moved except those who were close to Dave and Ted. Those men quickly moved back, away from these men who carried death in their hands.

Scott froze in his chair. His eyes protruded with amazement at his two fallen comrades. He studied Ted, uncertain for a moment who he was. When he saw Dave in the dark shadows, he knew who he was. He was The Ghost, the man from Abilene they had killed, the man who had never stopped hunting him. The black cigar fell from his white lips, and he groped backward out of his chair. He tripped over the body of one of his men, but the back wall of the cantina caught him. He remained hunched over and pressed against the wall, trembling with fear.

The metallic click of Dave and Ted reloading their rifles intensified the fearful silence.

Dave stepped toward the priest. He said softly in Spanish, "Move away from the boy, Padre."

The priest turned and tried to see the man in the shadows who spoke to him. All he saw under the brim of the hat was the burning hate that flowed from Dave's eyes. Ted watched the priest hesitate but finally move aside.

Dave held the stock of his Henry against his waist, with the barrel pointing up. He never took his eyes off Scott. He said to the boy in Spanish, "You were here first, señor. Do what you must."

The boy turned and looked up at Dave, not sure he understood, then nodded slightly. He faced Scott again. "Now I am indeed ready, terrible man."

Scott was not going to draw. He pushed his gun out of its holster, and it fell with a thump into the dirt by his feet. But he looked not at the boy, only at Dave.

The boy drew his gun, pulled back the hammer, and aimed it with both hands. His hands were steady, but he did not fire. Scott pleaded for mercy, and the boy dropped his arms, took a deep breath, and again took aim. The only sound in the cantina was Scott mumbling incoherently.

The boy dropped his arms again and turned toward Dave. "I cannot shoot even such a pig."

"I understand," Dave said in Spanish, without taking his eyes from Scott. "Do not grieve being unable to kill, even such an evil thing. His blood on your hands would have only brought you sorrow. You redeemed your family's honor when you faced him and his killers alone and unafraid."

The boy nodded at Dave that he understood. He went to the priest, who placed his hand approvingly on the boy's shoulder.

Scott stared at Dave and mumbled, "Who . . . who are you?"

"Kramer. Major Dave Kramer."

Scott said softly, "I don't have the gold."

"I know. I have it."

Scott looked puzzled.

"We met Sally Blackfoot on the Santa Fe Trail." Dave paused

and added, "Heading east with the gold after you left Loma Parda."

"She betrayed me. . . ." He shook his head angrily, then quickly composed himself and smiled evilly. He stood straight and smirked at Dave. "When you take me back, Major, I'll tell them you arrested me in Mexico, and they'll have to let me go. You can't arrest me in Mexico. The Army has no jurisdiction here." He stuck out his chin defiantly and waited for Dave to respond.

Dave didn't speak. He just let the Henry drop forward. Scott glanced at the rifle barrel pointed directly at him and then back at Dave's unblinking eyes. At that moment, Scott realized Dave was not there to take him back. He flung out his arms and started to scream as Dave and Ted opened fire at the same instant.

The force of the bullets smashed Jedd Scott against the adobe wall and held him there while one after another of the bullets ripped into him. When the rifles were finally empty, Scott crumpled slowly to the floor, the back wall a mosaic of blood and shattered adobe.

The Mexican people gasped. The priest crossed himself and mumbled, "The executioners of the Lord!"

No one moved as Dave and Ted reloaded, then turned and walked through the quickly formed aisle to their horses.

The Mexicans moved silently into the street and in fearful awe watched as the two horsemen of the Lord rode directly into the setting sun. They were legends before the sun's rays swallowed them.

Epilogue

They rode for a long time without speaking. Finally, Ted said, "I'm glad it's done. I'm truly glad it's finished."

Dave nodded. "Yeah, I know." He thought for a bit. "It's strange, but I don't feel the relief I thought I would. I kept hoping that once we'd killed Scott, all the hell would be over. Instead, it's just brought it all back to me. All the images of people I've loved and lost." Dave paused again. "I don't feel anything good. I just feel dirty."

The ride back to Quiet Valley would take four weeks. Dave decided that they should not rush the trip. He knew that they needed time for their minds to heal, for their spirits to mend. For the first time in too long, they were each free of the pain, anger, and rage that had driven them. For the first time they could dream of a future, of a new life, of women who loved them and they loved in return.

At the first stagecoach office, Ted sent a letter to Henrietta Byrne. Dave sent letters to his father, Elizabeth, and the Mc-Makins, letting them know that they were safe and heading home, that the hunt was over, that Jedd Scott was dead. The letters would arrive in less than a week, and it would take them three more weeks to get home.

They stopped at Fort Union, where Dave found that Colonel Willis had left just before Christmas and been replaced by Colonel Carson. Colonel Carson knew of Dave and his mission. He told Dave that he'd be sure Colonel Willis got word of Scott's demise.

While at Fort Union, Dave wrote letters to Captain Slim Filmore at Fort Livermore and Jim Bates at Wells Fargo and included letters to Doc and Red Whitfield for Jim Bates to forward. Lieutenant Bailey had just returned from an escort duty, and Dave convinced Colonel Carson to write him a two-day pass, much to Jerry's pleasure. They rode together to Loma Parda, where they spent two days resting with the alcalde.

The last days of travel, Dave and Ted were eager to get home, yet when they finally approached the back of the bank-hotel in the early dusk, Dave was reminded that the past was not always easily forgotten. He felt his muscles tighten. They had seen lights in a few houses along the ridge when they came over the pass, but memories of the last time he'd ridden home were still raw wounds that hadn't yet healed.

Ted glanced at Dave and saw the tension around his mouth as they rode around the bank and onto Main Street.

There were no empty buildings this time. Lights glowed cheerfully up and down the street. Dave glanced at Ted and smiled in relief. They rode tiredly toward the newspaper office.

A dirty-faced boy played on the sidewalk with a small, fat yellow puppy. A miner waved hello to them as he crossed the street. Dave's eyes absorbed it all with delight.

They rode to *The Quiet Valley Weekly* office, and a face appeared at the window, then two more. Dave's father, Elizabeth, and Henrietta rushed outside, yelling and laughing, and into the arms of two men who had ridden many hard miles for the joy of this moment.

Filing happily into the office, Dave paused for just a moment and looked up and down the street. Smiling contentedly, he stepped into the warm room and closed the door behind him.